# PASSION'S FIRE
### BY
## ANNA MARKLAND

**COVER ART BY STEVEN NOVAK**

Dedicated to a bright spark, my grandson, Peter

The stone's legacy is inescapable.
Those who inherit will be consumed by fire.

# DUBIOUS REWARD

*York Castle, England, 1175 AD*

Matthew de Rowenne couldn't have been any hotter if he'd been cast into the fires of hell.

Which he had.

"I'm to return to Scotland, Your Majesty?" he asked warily, lest he raise the ire of his volatile king. He fervently hoped the fury burning in his heart wasn't evident on his face. Filled with the relief of at last being recalled to England, he certainly hadn't anticipated being sent back north of the border. The grant of some small estate as a reward for his service was more what he'd had in mind, or at least a knighthood.

Several of the King's dozen advisors shifted their weight from one foot to the other, their leather boots squeaking on the tiled floor of the royal antechamber.

"Ranulf assures me you're the man for the job," King Henry Plantagenet replied, narrowing his blue-grey eyes. "You helped capture the upstart Scottish king at Alnwick last year during my son's rebellion." He turned to his advisors. "We quickly showed them where the true power lies."

To a man, they nodded in unison, agreeing heartily with the monarch's smug pronouncement.

Matthew risked a glance at Ranulf de Glanville. Few

could claim England's Chief Justiciar as a mentor. Only Henry wielded more power. Matthew was the second son of an obscure Anglo-Norman family—a nobody. It had been his great good fortune to have aided Ranulf in the capture of William the Lion in Northumbria. His unhorsing of the Scottish king that day had brought him to the famous warrior's attention. "I am as always deeply humbled by the faith my lord Ranulf has in me," he tried, "and it was a distinct honor to escort King William to imprisonment in Falaise, but—"

Henry waved him to silence as if shooing away a pesky gnat. He was clearly losing patience, his always florid face turning as red as his hair. Everyone recognised the bloodshot eyes as a clear indication he'd been away from his hunting addiction for over an hour. He'd arrived late, clad in riding attire. "The treaty is ratified and the Scots king has sworn fealty to me," he declared in his gravelly voice, thrusting out his leonine head. "Hopefully my Scottish cousin has learned his lesson."

While the assembled courtiers grunted their agreement with the regal optimism, Matthew's attention drifted to memories of his visit to Falaise. It had been a challenge escorting a humiliated king in chains across the Narrow Sea, but it had brought him close to Montbryce Castle, seat of his ancestral family on his mother's side. He'd trained as a page there, then as a squire. Normandie was the place of his birth and the fortnight spent at Montbryce had reminded him again of how much he loved his native land. Though he was an offshoot of a minor branch of the family, the Montbryces always treated him with respect. He thirsted to rise to the higher echelons of Norman nobility.

But his older brother had inherited the small de Rowenne estate, forcing Matthew to earn his living as a mercenary. The de Rowenne holdings weren't substantial. It was family lore that their medieval patriarch had been a Frankish weapon-smith.

Ranulf coughed loudly, jolting Matthew back to the antechamber. Surely the king hadn't just said—

"You've proven by your exploits with the army I sent north after William's capture that you know how to subdue dissident barbaric factions," Henry shouted.

The counsellors shifted their gaze from the king to Matthew, as if they were watching a *jeu de paume*. He cleared his throat while he considered his response. It would be useless, and probably imprudent, to retort that he'd found the Scottish court a surprisingly cultured place. But the ancient town of Scone didn't seem to be the destination the monarch had in mind on this occasion.

"The king has granted William the Lion permission to return to Scotland," Ranulf announced. "It's to be expected his pledge of fealty to the English Crown has stirred unrest in certain regions. There are renewed rumblings of discontent and rebellion in the so-called Kingdom of Galloway," he added with some sarcasm. "Castles must be built in the area. You will assist the Scottish king to bring these wandering sheep into his fold."

Matthew racked his brain. Where in the name of all the saints was Galloway?

"It's imperative we gain control of a region on our northwestern border," the Chief Justiciar continued.

"Gilbride MacFergus is already overrunning the Scottish king's defences there. It's a threat to Carlisle."

The counsellors mumbled their consternation at this possibility. Carlisle was after all where King David had knighted Henry long ago during the Civil War.

Matthew deemed it curious that the folk of Galloway evidently didn't want to be Scots.

Henry was already on his feet, heading for the door, shoving his big, rough hands into leather gauntlets. Matthew surmised he was off to play with his hawks. The king was fond of boasting that was the only time he ever wore gloves.

He breathed a little easier. At least he wasn't being sent to the barren Highlands. All heads bowed as the energetic monarch strode towards the door with his bowlegged gait. But he turned unexpectedly and winked. "Oh, and I've instructed Ranulf to find you a bride in Galloway. Such alliances make for peaceful relations."

Utter silence greeted this nonsensical declaration. The King's marriage to Eleanor of Aquitaine had resulted in years of civil strife among his children. Henry's Council hurried out after him, leaving Matthew alone in the empty chamber.

Summarily being ordered to return to Scotland filled him with impotent fury and indignation, but the king was well aware he was a second son with no responsibilities to keep him in England.

Being an officer in an invading army was fraught with dangers. The prospect of keeping the peace now the Scottish king had been humiliated and forced to cede lands, castles and authority to the English king was daunting. The Scots would be in uproar if they were obliged to pay taxes to support the occupying English army.

As if those obstacles weren't enough, there were folk in the northern wastelands who apparently didn't want to be Scots. Their origins must lay elsewhere.

Henry apparently had confidence in Matthew's abilities to calm the troubled waters and he resolved to do his utmost to carry out the mission entrusted to him. Eventually the king would reward him.

Marriage, however, was out of the question.

He fingered the blood red glass set in the cross-shaped pin that held his woollen cloak in place. A Frankish ancestor had acquired it long ago. A Latin palindrome was engraved into the glass. It was his legacy, the only thing of value traditionally passed on to the second son.

He supposed that three hundred years ago such amusing palindromes had been the fashion. They were the same no matter which way you read them. *In girum imus nocte et consumimur igni*. The clever humor was completely lost in his own language; *we go around in circles at night and are consumed by fire*. But the engraver had the humble moth in mind when he conceived the riddle, and that still held true in any language. Moths drawn to fly in circles around a flame were quickly consumed.

However, the legacy had proven to be a curse. The wives of the last three de Rowennes to possess the brooch had all perished by fire, his own mother included.

Marriage to Matthew carried a ghastly death sentence.

# BRIG

Brigandine had been a boy for as long as she could remember.

Her mother had died when she was a babe in arms. Grieving the loss of his first wife, and seemingly unable to sire children with his unlamented shrewish second partner, Gorrie Lordsmith had been obliged to recruit his daughter as his assistant.

Almost before she could walk she learned how to rekindle the forge fire, blow into the tubes to keep the embers hot, and the smithy swept clean of debris that might catch fire. However, girls didn't apprentice to sword-smiths. In desperation her Da had dressed her in boy's clothing and kept her hair shorn. From the start he'd taken to calling her Brig. Some days she believed he'd completely forgotten she was a girl. Most days she forgot it herself.

At the time of her birth, word had reached his ears of the *brigandine*, a new style of plated mailcoat made in such a way to allow for easier movement. Impressed by the idea and certain the Arabic design would eventually reach Galloway, he'd insisted his daughter be named in its honor. He'd spent the seventeen years since trying to produce something comparable.

6

Her father's fine handiwork in fashioning and repairing weapons and armor eventually came to the attention of Gilbride MacFergus, Lord of Galloway.

Gorrie became Gilbride's armorer and his arrival at MacFergus's stronghold at Cruggleton caused no more than a brief stir. Everyone assumed his apprentice was a boy.

Brig loved the intense heat of the fire on her face, the sweat trickling down her back, the smell of burning wood, the magical spread of the red hot glow in the heated metal. Working in the forge was better than being shut up in Lincluden Abbey with the nuns, and certainly preferable to slaving in the castle's kitchen or laundry.

Her father had plied his trade in Gilbride's western stronghold at Cruggleton. They'd only recently been obliged to follow their Lord to Lincluden, seat of Uchtred MacFergus, co-ruler of Galloway and brother to Gilbride. No one at Lincluden had any reason to suspect she was a girl.

A MacFergus family gathering was not the reason for Gilbride's visit. He summarily blinded and castrated Uchtred, cutting out his brother's tongue for good measure. As far as anyone knew the wretch was dead.

"Better we have one leader," her father declared for the umpteenth time since Uchtred's murder. He prodded the burning logs with the poker. "More chance of fending off them Scots."

Brig sensed he was trying to come to terms with the shocking turn of events. "But our champion has fled back to Cruggleton now the Scots king is on his way with an English army at his beck and call," she retorted, gripping the rough wooden lever of the bellows. She had to be alert for the moment air would be needed to kindle sufficient heat.

Though taller than she when they'd first been installed, the bellows were a welcome improvement over the foul tasting air tubes. As she'd grown, her father had adjusted the length of the lever, but it still took strength to force air out of the giant machine. Transporting the huge double bellows from Cruggleton had been a feat. That was also the reason they'd remained in Lincluden and not fled with Gilbride. Gorrie was convinced his master would return.

Brig wasn't so sure, though she fervently hoped he was right. She feared Gilbride, but had no desire for her homeland to be swallowed up into the Scottish kingdom. Her ancestors were Vikings, her language and customs different from those of the Scots. Her people had prospered for generations without foreign interference.

"There's trouble abrewin'," Gorrie muttered, jolting her thoughts back to the forge. "Mark my words, laddie."

Brig was prevented from replying by the deafening ring of his sledgehammer striking the steel ingot he was fashioning into a sword. She seized the opportunity of the brief respite to wipe the sweat from her brow and swig a mouthful of water from the dipper.

"Keep that flame aburnin' bright, laddie," her father admonished.

Confident he had exhausted his arsenal of conversation, Brig resumed her post behind the bellows and put her back into forcing air into the forge fire.

Being a man and plying a man's trade had its benefits. Her father would never have allowed a girl to express opinions about Gilbride, or about anything that went on in Galloway. The work had made her strong. Some might think her too muscled for a lass, but she didn't care. She liked being a lad. The maidservants and peasant women of her acquaintance talked of nothing but marriage. However, it seemed to her what they sought was a protector, a provider. She didn't need protection. Her father had taught her well; she knew how to use the weapons he fashioned. He told her she was a gifted swordsman, but she doubted that was true.

She roamed freely, usually unaccompanied. No one challenged the dirty urchin with the tufts of red hair. No one cared.

"Aye, trouble," Gorrie mumbled again to her surprise. "Uchtred, God rest his soul, would ha' made peace wi' them Normans in England, formed an alliance agin' King William the Lion, so we could stay out o' Scotland's clutches."

Her Da's unusual willingness to share thoughts that if overheard might result in his death gave her confidence. "But Gilbride isna in favor o' Normans," she replied.

Gorrie shook his head, his eyes fixed all the while on the glowing ingot trapped in the firm grip of the iron tongs. Its slowly changing shape fascinated Brig. "Nay. Despises 'em as much as he hates the Scots. When he heard of William's capture at Alnwick he slaughtered the bailiffs and guards the king of Scotland had set over us."

Brig recalled the lead weight that had lain in her belly

when news had reached them of Gilbride's reign of terror.

While she shared her father's pride in the beautifully crafted weapons he manufactured, to her mind they should be used for defence, not for brutal maiming, torture and slaughter.

"I s'pose Uchtred wasna in favor of the killin'," she ventured. "That's why Gilbride did away wi' him."

To her surprise, her Da stopped hammering and stared at her, his dirty face streaked with rivulets of sweat. "We musna say too much. But mark my words, Brig, trouble will come. The Plantagenet English king willna allow Gilbride to control Galloway. 'Tis too close to Cumbria and their stronghold in Carlisle."

This was the first time he'd shared his fears. She too feared what lay ahead, but sought to reassure him. She scooped water from the bucket and handed him the dipper. "Dinna worry, Da. We'll stay out of their way and let them get on with their struggles. When all's said and done, they'll always need an armorer."

Gorrie slurped greedily, then wiped a dirty forearm across his brow. A rare smile tugged at the corners of his mouth.

She was glad she'd lightened his load, but her words didn't ring true in her own ears. She didn't have it in her to sit back and do nothing when all she loved was under threat.

# CARLISLE

*Carlisle Castle, Cumbria*

Matthew was an accomplished horseman. His Norman forebears were members of the legendary cavalry that turned the tide at Hastings in William the Conqueror's favor. Riding was in his blood.

However, he was happy to dismount from his faithful Belenus after three tough days traversing the Pennines as second-in-command of a sizeable army. The sight of Carlisle's tall tower was welcome indeed after miles of bleak and barren moorland, relieved only by clumps of bracken and heather.

However, the Pennine hares were plump and tasty. At the end of long days in the saddle, the becks and streams provided a chance to cleanse away the dust and sweat, despite the icy lick of the water.

Carlisle, northwestern outpost of King Henry's kingdom, was already crammed with English soldiers. The Scots had laid siege more than once in recent years. Matthew's superior officer, Blaise Le Cordier, negotiated with the Castellan for their mercenary *routiers* to camp alongside the River Eden. However, the remainder of their regular army would set up their tents on the other side of the castle on the banks of the Caldew.

The plan was to keep the troublemaking mercenaries from Brabant and Aragon out of harm's way. They'd already instigated violent arguments on the journey, resulting in three deaths. Matthew was, as usual, put in charge of the *routier* camp.

Le Cordier, a career officer descended from a noble family named in the Domesday Book, despised the mercenaries. Matthew recognised in many of them the frustrations of young men obliged to earn their keep by putting their lives in constant danger for the highest bidder. Far from homes they hadn't seen in years, surrounded by people who didn't speak their language, hated by the very foreign masters who employed them, they stuck together, though the worst violence was usually between the Brabançons and the Aragonese.

The hostility of the hot-tempered Spaniards in particular increased as the air chilled in the Pennines. However, for some reason, the hired soldiers respected Matthew, if grudgingly. He supposed they recognised he too was landless, forced to earn his living through warfare. He praised the saints every day for the stroke of luck that had enabled him to unhorse William the Lion. His subsequent speedy rise through the ranks had saved him from the life the *routiers* led. The Norman blood in his veins helped. He had only to mention he was a descendant of the Montbryce family to see disdain turn to respect. Even the haughty Le Cordier had suddenly become talkative and friendly.

He never mentioned his Frankish ancestry. Weapon-smithing didn't carry a lot of weight with men like Le Cordier.

On the journey he'd learned a great deal about

Galloway from his Commander. "Norse-Gaels," the arrogant Norman explained, hacking up and spitting out phlegm. "*Ostmen*, they call themselves."

"From the East?" Matthew queried.

"*Oui*, although they are mostly descended from Vikings who settled in Ireland and the land of the Gaels, or from folk they conquered."

Matthew stifled an urge to snort. Normans were proud descendants of Vikings who'd migrated to the valley of the Seine, yet Le Cordier spoke of the Norsemen as if they were barbarians. It was highly likely his own ancestors were Vikings.

"Consider themselves too good to be subjects of the King of Scotland," Le Cordier said with great sarcasm. "Ironic we're now going to help the Lion regain control of them."

Satisfied all was well in the camp, Matthew eased off his best boots and settled onto his camp-cot, listening to the raucous singing and dancing of the Aragonese. It occurred to him he probably had more in common with the people of Galloway than he did with King Henry. The monarch touted his descent from Norman kings, but his father had been a hated Angevin, Jeffrey Plantagenet, and the recently humiliated king of Scotland was his own cousin. Henry was helping William gain control of Galloway because he controlled William.

Matthew resolved to tread warily. Two days hence they would venture into Galloway to establish an English presence in the name of the Scots king Matthew had personally taken in chains to Normandie. Loyalties could shift quickly, like treacherous tidal sands.

# THE SHEARING

*Lincluden Castle, Galloway*

"I'll nay argue with ye further," Gorrie declared. "Either ye cut yer hair, or we forget the scheme. The Plantagenet king's army is only an hour away. If ye want to carry on as my apprentice—"

Exasperated, Brig tore off the tam under which she'd tucked her lengthening hair. "I'd a notion to grow it into a queue," she protested. She didn't want to reveal she'd caught a glimpse of herself in a maidservant's mirror and been aghast at the red tufts sprouting from her head. No wonder the castle's maids went into fits of giggles whenever they set eyes on her.

Gorrie chuckled, eyeing her up and down. "Nay. A queue would make ye look too much like a young lordling."

He closed one eye, a frown wrinkling his already furrowed brow.

"What is it?" she asked nervously.

Her father studied his feet. "Ye mun do summat wi' yer womanly parts," he rasped, his ruddy face redder than usual. "They're gettin' bigger, and there's an army o' men on the way."

She looked down at her breasts. When they'd first started to grow, she'd concealed them by wearing more voluminous shirts. But her Da had the right of it. Working in the forge had developed more than just the muscles in her arms and legs. "I'll cut my old shirts into strips for binding."

Her father seemed satisfied and went back to hammering. It was important he carry on his craft when the invaders came. An army needed someone capable of repairing weapons and armor. There was no finer craftsman in the whole of Galloway than Gorrie Lordsmith. The invasion might prove to be a godsend. As a youth she'd be able to come and go at will and spy on the enemy whereas the unwed girls of Lincluden were secreted away in the Abbey.

Resigned to the inevitable shearing, she turned her back and perched on the edge of the low stone wall of the smithy. "Do yer worst," she sighed, the tam clutched in her grip.

Gorrie brandished his spring scissors and took hold of a length of hair. He hesitated, causing her to glance up at him. He was wiping away a tear with the back of his hand. "Eh, lass," he said hoarsely, "I wish this wasna necessary. Yer Ma's likely turnin' o'er in her grave. Forgive me."

It was the first time he'd ever uttered such a notion. She put a hand on his arm. "'Twill grow again. Dinna fash."

"Someday ye'll boast lovely tresses down to yer waist," he rasped. "Like yer Ma."

The prospect was alarming. Her Da reminisced often about her mother's long chestnut tresses. According to him, long hair attracted men, and she'd no wish to do that. She screwed her eyes tight shut, fighting back tears as the steel chewed into her hair. By the time he was done, her scalp ached. She ran a hand over the tufts. The metallic crunch of the sharpened blades had again robbed her of the one thing of beauty she might possess. But that was a foolish notion. Anxious to remove the sadness from her father's face, she smiled weakly and gathered the shorn locks from the ground. "Best to burn it," she murmured.

"Aye," he mumbled.

They watched as the flames consumed in moments what had taken sennights to grow.

"Now to make bindings," she said, flattening her breasts with her palms.

His face reddened further. "I canna help ye with that."

# FIRST MEETING

There was no marker to indicate the army had passed into Galloway, but Matthew knew it when harassment from unseen skirmishers began. Rocks bounced off byrnies, raising the ire of men who marched in armor in unseasonably hot weather. Some Aragonese became particularly incensed and it took considerable persuasion to prevent them pursuing the culprits. "It's what they want," Matthew yelled. "Once you're isolated they'll cut you down."

He reprimanded them for shooting crossbow bolts at the unseen enemy. Ammunition was too costly to waste. It was a relief the attackers didn't seem to have the deadly weapons. Stones might bruise and mayhap even break a bone, but they were unlikely to be lethal.

Undergrowth had to be cut back as they made their way through forests to the River Nith. Once they reached the river, the going became boggy as sunny skies gave way to torrential rain.

Matthew thanked God for his horse. As always, the animal took it all in stride, seemingly knowing what his master wanted even before he did. To the casual observer, Belenus probably seemed like a placid, obedient horse. Matthew knew the fiery spirit lurking within that could spark to life when called upon, as it had when he'd unhorsed William. It was the reason he'd named the steed for the Celtic god of fire.

Le Cordier had decided Lincluden Castle would be the base from where they would scout the Nith, searching for the best place to construct a large castle to control access to the sea and the hinterland. Word had come that King William was of the opinion Lincluden itself was too far north and too old to form the basis of a strong fortress. Once Matthew set eyes on the dilapidated castle he suspected William simply wanted something grander. But at least the rain had stopped.

They'd expected more opposition, but none came as they rode at last into the small bailey, after passing what looked like an abbey on the way.

"Not a soul about," Le Cordier declared, scanning the deserted bailey.

Matthew looked around. It was too quiet. Was it simply that the local inhabitants intended to show displeasure at their arrival, or was it a trap?

Even the boisterous *routiers* hushed as hundreds of men tensed, listening for the slightest sound that might indicate trouble.

Tired horses snorted. Steam rose from puddles of rainwater as the sun gained a foothold in the sky. From some distant place a sound reached their ears. A rhythmic pounding. Metal on metal.

It dawned on Matthew his heart was beating in cadence with what sounded like a hammer. "A forge, I believe," he said to the frowning Commander.

Le Cordier's face brightened. "*Bon!* We'll need the services of a smith."

~~~

It was Brig's suggestion they keep the forge working, though the rest of the castle's inhabitants had either secreted themselves indoors, or fled into the countryside. "It will bring us to their attention," she insisted to her reluctant father. "They will know immediately there is a smith here."

Her heart, already thudding with every blow of her Da's hammer, raced erratically when two enemy soldiers trotted around the corner of the undercroft where the forge was located. That they were mounted spoke of their rank. They were both tall and broad in the shoulders, heavily armored, their faces half hidden by their helmets. Exactly what she'd expected.

She forced herself to pump the bellows, though it was unlikely they would notice a mere lad. As she'd hoped, they watched her father. Nervous pride filled her when he carried on his task as if they weren't there.

One of the soldiers shouted something. His manner was arrogant and though she didn't understand his words, she suspected it was French he spoke. This was no doubt the superior of the two. He bristled when Gorrie ignored him, his face reddening as he looked to the other man.

"Blacksmith," the second soldier shouted.

Despite the heat of the forge, a shiver trickled up Brig's spine. Not only had he spoken in the language of the Gaels, but something about his voice tightened her throat. Unlike the other man he seemed amused.

The urge was to correct his pronunciation and then to protest that her Da wasn't a mere blacksmith, but that would draw attention she didn't want.

Gorrie thrust the ingot back into the hot embers, lay down the hammer and turned slowly, wiping his hands on the blackened cloth hanging from his leather apron. He bowed slightly, just enough, she thought, to appease the first man's ruffled feathers. "I'm not a blacksmith, my lords," he said politely. "I'm the armorer."

This seemed to please the first man. The scowl left his face as he replied. The second man translated what he'd said. "We are in need of an armorer."

To her surprise, the soldier who seemed to know a few words of her language dismounted, drawing her attention to his horse. It was an unusual reddish brown color.

"I am Matthew de Rowenne," he said, "and my Commander is *Capitaine* Le Cordier."

The captain dismounted, but she barely noticed, so taken was she with the red horse.

"You there, lad."

She blinked. Surely de Rowenne wasn't speaking to her. She dug her nails into the wood, suddenly realizing she'd forgotten to put on her leather gloves.

He held out the reins. "Your master's fire needs no more air. See to our horses."

She stumbled forward, stubbing her little toe on the stone platform on which the bellows sat. Tears welled as pain throbbed. Trying unsuccessfully to stop the trembling in her hands, she took hold of the reins of both horses, her gaze fixed on the reddening toe.

De Rowenne chuckled. "Don't you know you should always wear shoes in a smithy," he said softly.

She glanced up sharply into ice blue eyes full of amusement. She wanted to kick him in a place she knew would hurt because other boys had told her so. How did this arrogant Norman know when a fire needed more air? She clenched her jaw and averted her gaze, her eyes drawn to the blood red glass of the brooch that secured his cloak. Symbols had been engraved into it. It looked old and valuable. Probably bought with wages paid by his English king.

But his interest in her was fleeting. "Take good care of our horses," he said sternly, waving her away with a gloved hand.

She was about to retort that she wasn't a stable boy when he winked and whispered, "Especially Belenus. He's special."

Belenus? God of fire? The knot in her belly loosened. It was the perfect name for the horse. She'd never ridden in her life but suddenly wanted to leap on the animal's back and gallop away.

The Captain had entered the smithy and was examining some of the weaponry her father had made. He seemed particularly interested in the brigandine mailshirts hanging from the rafters that Gorrie had attempted to perfect. De Rowenne joined them, acting as interpreter.

She led the horses to the stables, wondering where he'd learned to speak her language. Her resentment of him eased. At least the man knew a thing or two about naming horses. But she was strangely irritated that he hadn't asked her name.

# ODD

*Odd.*

Matthew couldn't get the thought out of his mind.

The armorer's lad was odd.

Why it preoccupied him, he didn't know.

He joined Le Cordier in the smithy, but barely paid attention to the well-crafted weapons, though the mailed jacket was intriguing. If the armorer ever perfected it—

Belenus had certainly snared the youth's attention.

He chuckled when he remembered the reddening toe. He was sure the urchin wanted to curse, but he'd kept silent.

There was something odd about the lad's feet, and the trembling hands, but he couldn't put his finger on what it was.

The apprentice was likely terrified. Judging by what he'd heard of goings-on at Lincluden Castle, how was anyone to feel safe there? A man who mutilated and murdered his own brother would do away with an armorer's apprentice without batting an eyelid.

He shrugged off his worries. He had bigger problems to take care of, an army to billet, the *routiers* to control, a plan to devise for scouting the environs, guards to be posted. They'd have to unearth the servants, get the castle going, reassure them they were safe if they obeyed.

And the tufts of red hair! The armorer must have taken his shears to the lad's head. He wondered if the youth was the man's son.

"*Bon*," Le Cordier said decisively. "Tell him I am impressed with his work. See that any weapons in need of repair are sent to him. He is to give his full attention to our needs. However, if he has spare time he can continue his experiments with the mail shirt."

He strode off, leaving Matthew with the armorer who nodded his understanding of what was expected of him. A thought occurred. "What is your name?"

"Gorrie," the man replied. "Gorrie Lordsmith."

Matthew arched a brow. "You were weapon-smith to MacFergus?"

"I was," Gorrie responded proudly.

"And your son's name?"

Why he'd asked, he didn't know. But the man suddenly looked sheepish and shifted his considerable weight from one foot to the other. He dabbed his forehead with the filthy cloth tied to his apron.

"He is your son, is he not?"

"Brig. His name is Brig," Gorrie finally replied, resuming his hammering as the sullen lad reappeared from the stables and took up his post at the bellows.

*Odd name*, Matthew thought. *Must be Gaelic.*

He set off in search of Le Cordier. There was much to be done and his *Capitaine* would no doubt expect him to do it.

~~~

Brig cursed, thankful the arrogant soldier with the

wondrous horse had left them alone. Why hadn't she worn her shoes? She never went barefoot in the smithy. Even the Norman knew it was foolhardy, and the last thing she wanted him to look at was her feet. They were too small for a tall youth.

And the gloves. She always wore them.

She resolved to be more careful. No one in the invading army must uncover her secret. Her father's livelihood had been at stake before, but now her life depended on the ruse. Who knew what kind of men lurked in the rank and file of the English army?

As if to bear out her fears, a long line of weary looking infantrymen appeared in the distance, heading for the fields on the banks of the Nith.

Gorrie stopped hammering. "They'll set up camp near the river," he said.

The Nith was where she drew their water. "I'll have to fetch water from the Cluden instead," she said.

Gorrie narrowed his eyes. "I doubt we're seeing the whole army. I'd guess some will camp by the Cluden too. Dinna worry. I'll refill the water-skins."

It pained her to make more work for her Da, but she was grateful he'd sensed her fear.

"Ye did the right thing, Brig. Keep silent. Say naught. Give them no reason to suspect. We do their bidding while we watch and wait."

*But what are we waiting for?* she wondered, distracted by loud shouting coming from the fields.

Gorrie shaded his eyes with his hand. "Looks like a dispute. Lots of pushing and shoving. Probably mercenaries."

Brig shuddered. She'd never heard anything good

about mercenary soldiers who were reputed to owe loyalty to no one but themselves.

As the brawl escalated, Matthew de Rowenne strode into the midst of the melee. A hammer pounded in Brig's head. "They'll tear him to pieces," she murmured.

After only a few minutes, the ruckus quieted. Men went back to pitching tents. De Rowenne stood watch, arms folded across his chest.

"He's got the measure of that mob," her Da said.

She snorted. "Sounds like ye admire him for it," she scoffed.

He picked up his hammer. "And ye sounded like ye cared if they turned on him."

"Nay," she protested. "I just dinna like brutality. Ye know that."

He looked at her curiously for a moment then resumed his hammering.

Working the bellows, she gazed out to the field. Matthew de Rowenne looked rather splendid standing calmly while his unruly minions set up the camp. There was more to the man than met the eye.

# ANNAN

"The Nith might not be the best location for a castle," Le Cordier declared. "I have reports the Annan also empties into the Solway and its mouth is closer to Carlisle."

They'd gone back and forth over this ground for two days. Matthew privately thought the Nith was a better choice. Any seagoing threat to Scottish control of Galloway would likely sail up the Solway and encounter the Nith first. A fortification just south of Lincluden, in his opinion, would provide faster access to the Solway.

Their mission was to build a defensive position to protect Galloway, not Carlisle, from Gilbride. The Lord of Galloway surely wouldn't risk launching an attack close to Henry's Cumbrian stronghold.

However, Le Cordier had so far not proven himself to be a man tolerant of anything other than his own opinion, therefore Matthew said nothing.

"*Bon.* I've made my decision. Take a contingent of *routiers* and scout the Annan," his *Capitaine* commanded.

Matthew was tempted to roll his eyes. He might have known Le Cordier would assign troublemakers to the task instead of regular army. But he had to keep the prize in mind. Henry wouldn't grant land or a knighthood to a soldier who challenged his commanding officer.

"I'll pick out some of the Aragonese," he replied. "Shouldn't take more than a fortnight to get the lay of the land."

Le Cordier fiddled with the end of his moustache. "Be thorough. Meanwhile we'll explore the valley of the Nith. And take some locals with you who know the area. It will save time."

Few able-bodied men were to be found in the castle. Matthew suspected locals had been among the stone throwing skirmishers. The armorer would be an asset on such an expedition, but he was needed at Lincluden.

"Take the lad from the smithy," his commander suggested.

Matthew was taken aback. The notion was strangely appealing at first, but he realized he hadn't really thought of Brig as an able-bodied youth, though the lad was tall and strong looking as well as odd.

"Who will help the armorer?" he replied.

"Don't be concerned with that. I can easily find a Brabanter to pump bellows."

Matthew felt a momentary pang of pity for the armorer obliged to work with a troublemaking *routier*, but who else was there? He'd have to warn the lad to stay out of the way of the Spaniards. Brig was the kind of victim they took pleasure in picking on.

~~~

Brig perched on the low stone wall surrounding the smithy, fretting over her father's mounting frustration. The foreign lout assigned to work the bellows seemed to have the brains of an ox. He had the muscles for the job, which was the root of the problem. He was putting too much force into his effort, sending flames leaping in the air that nigh on scorched Gorrie's eyebrows. She anticipated before much time passed, sparks would fly, and not just from the fire.

She'd been given no choice about joining the expedition to the Annan. It was comical since she'd never been further east than Lincluden and had little idea how to get to the eastern river. She'd have to rely on asking locals if her father's directions proved wrong.

The prospect of travelling with a band of armed men filled her with dread, and yet she was strangely excited. De Rowenne would be mounted on Belenus, a horse she loved. She'd snuck into the stable at every opportunity to pet the animal. The red horse seemed to like her.

The Norman had mentioned his contingent would be made up of Spaniards and advised her to avoid them. She intended to do just that. But he'd also told her to stick close to his side. That presented a problem. She found she liked him, despite his foreign ways. The first time she'd seen him without his helmet, she'd been struck by how attractive he was, his handsome face framed by long hair as black as night.

But if she got too close, he might discover her true identity.

She studied her boots. When they'd travelled from Cruggleton she'd ridden in the wagon with the paraphernalia from the forge. She hoped her worn leather footwear would stand up to miles of walking. Da had given her a sturdy satchel with a long strap. It contained a flask of water and some bread and cheese.

He'd assured her de Rowenne's men would snare and cook food on the way, so carrying excess weight would bog her down needlessly. She'd slung it across her body, though not before secreting within it a dagger, and two small apples from the root-cellar for Belenus.

Da lamented over and over that he didn't want her to go, but they had no choice.

Her heart leapt into her throat when de Rowenne emerged out of the dawn mist that clung to the field, leading a band of twenty or so scowling foot soldiers, all swarthy. They put her in mind of a pack of cowed dogs she'd seen often in Cruggleton. Gilbride's dogs if she remembered correctly.

The prospect of marching miles on foot with these men made her knees tremble. She inhaled deeply and squared her shoulders. She was a lad, not some weak lass.

She rose from the wall and walked purposefully towards the Spaniards.

"Where are you going?" de Rowenne asked, his hand held out.

She frowned in confusion.

"You cannot march with them. They are used to it. You're not." He smiled the crooked smile she'd become used to seeing. "Besides, you have a sore toe, my lad."

She risked a glance at the Spaniards.

"Don't worry. They're Aragonese. They don't understand what we are saying," he reassured her. "Come. You'll ride behind me. Le Cordier refuses to spare a horse for you."

March with brutes or ride behind Matthew de

Rowenne on his magical steed? The choice was clear. "I have never ridden before," she said.

The Norman narrowed his eyes. "I think those are the first words I've heard you utter, Brig."

That was worrisome. Had she spoken like a girl?

"Mayhap you're learning not to fear me? Stand on the wall and I'll heave you up," he said with a smile.

She breathed again. He'd noticed nothing odd.

She took his hand. His heat came as a shock. She wished she'd worn her gloves, but they were jammed onto the Brabanter's meaty fists. For a brief second their eyes met. She couldn't look away. Something in the blue depths of his gaze held her.

She struggled clumsily into the space behind him, hefting the satchel onto her back. She reached behind to grip the edge of the saddle, appreciating immediately why noblewomen rode side-saddle. The leather pressed firmly on her most private place.

Over the years it had been unavoidable to occasionally glimpse other lads' male parts. She supposed they grew as they became adults, just like her breasts had grown. How did a big man like de Rowenne fare astride a horse? It had to be uncomfortable, though he seemed at ease atop Belenus.

Her feet dangled, her thighs touched de Rowenne's arse—no choice. It was very unladylike. She came close to snorting out loud at the notion. She wasn't a lady. Notwithstanding her masquerade as a youth, she was the daughter of a sword-smith.

The snort turned to a muffled *Oh!* as the horse moved forward and the leather of the saddle rubbed against that intimate place. It was a peculiar sensation.

"Hold on to my hips, lad," de Rowenne said curtly as they rode out of the bailey. "Don't want you tumbling to the ground."

The prospect of falling beneath the feet of the Spaniards was enough to make her comply. Reluctantly, she put her hands on his hips, gripping the folds of his cloak.

For the first mile or two she bounced uncomfortably, though they were travelling slowly to allow the infantry to keep up. By the time they reached the Annan she'd have blisters on her bottom.

"Relax," de Rowenne said over his shoulder. "Lean against me. Feel Belenus's gait."

She couldn't see his face, but his tone of voice told her he was smiling. He was right. She had to relax. There was naught to fear from Matthew de Rowenne. She leaned against his back, reassured by the solid strength she found there. She wondered if all men carried the musky scent that filled her nostrils.

It crossed her mind briefly that mayhap it was a mistake to trust this man. But better him that the wolfpack loping along behind them.

# UNDER ATTACK

Matthew fidgeted with the brooch pinned into the folds of his cloak, half expecting the red glass to be hot to the touch.

He'd ridden a horse since he was child and never felt discomfort in the groin area. Probably because he couldn't recall ever riding with a rock hard arousal before.

He'd heard tell of men who consorted with boys. They lived life in the shadows, constantly in fear of persecution if their proclivities came to light. His blood ran cold at the notion he might be among them. How else to explain the strange excitement that had crept over him as Brig's slight body rubbed against his back.

Since his mother's death he'd been determined not to allow his male urges to lead him into a relationship with a woman. Mayhap he'd suppressed his physical needs too often. He'd begun the day confident in his masculinity. Now he feared—

He swallowed hard, unwilling to even contemplate the terrifying possibility.

Brig's hands still rested on his hips, warm thighs pressed against his arse, but he'd a feeling the lad had nodded off. He was desperate to ease his discomfort, but he might startle the boy if he shifted his position in the saddle. He didn't want him falling beneath the feet of the Aragonese whose surly dispositions hadn't improved after a half hour on the march.

Only a half hour. They'd just forded the Nith. By the saints he'd be a wreck by the time they reached the Annan. There was even something arousing about the lad's smell.

A chill raced through his veins when Brig unexpectedly slouched further forward and snaked his arms around Matthew's waist. He looked down at the lad's hands. They were—appealing.

By the saints! He didn't dare turn around. Hopefully the Aragonese hadn't noticed anything amiss. If they suspected his aberrant thoughts, he was lost.

Suddenly, a hue and cry went up from the Spaniards.

Brig startled and gripped his shoulders. "Stones," he cried.

Matthew turned Belenus, worried the boy had been struck. What he saw knotted his gut. A horde of half naked men were rushing down a nearby hillside towards them, yelling a bloodthirsty battle cry.

"Gaels," he shouted to the infantrymen. "Take up your positions."

The attackers outnumbered his party, but the Aragonese were fierce, disciplined soldiers when it came to a fight. They quickly fell into formation, crossbows aimed at the oncoming marauders. A few of the Gaels had shortbows, but most seemed to be armed with stones and farm implements.

He had to get Brig to safety. The lad was no warrior. Espying a rocky outcropping, he galloped towards it. "Stay here," he yelled. "We'll soon finish them off.

They're just Gaels."

As Brig slid to the ground, his face white with fear, their gazes met. "I'm a Gael," he rasped.

~~~

Trembling, Brig sat with her back to the rough rock, rummaging desperately in her satchel for the dagger. Why couldn't she find it? There was barely anything in the—

She gulped down a sob when her hand settled on the hilt. She cast the satchel aside and held the weapon to her breast, deafened by her own heartbeat. It was likely Matthew's well trained soldiers would carry the day, but if they didn't she wouldn't die without a fight.

The irony of it. Killed by her own people.

She touched her temple where the stone had struck, upset when her fingers came away sticky with blood. She'd been enjoying the comforting warmth of de Rowenne's broad back when the attack had taken her off guard.

She blinked rapidly, wanting to be rid of the vision behind her eyes. Naked men armed with pitchforks rushing headlong into crossbow bolts shot by men in chainmail. What were they thinking? The hopelessness of the fight against the combined English and Scottish army struck her like a blow to the belly. With King Henry's help, William the Lion would swoop Galloway into his talons like the eagle fishing for salmon in the Nith.

Unless Gilbride organised his forces and put a stop to this kind of senseless marauding by disparate groups of peasants, Galloway was doomed.

It came to her that the harsh sounds of fighting had

ceased. Judging by the jubilant shouts in Spanish, the Aragonese had carried the day. Her heart lurched. Had Matthew survived, had he been injured? She struggled to her feet, still clutching the dagger, a troubling thought gnawing her. Why did she care, and when had she started to think of him as Matthew?

What she saw when she peered over the rock broke her heart. Injured, dead or dying men lay at the base of the hillock. All Gaels. They hadn't even made it to the road. Tears welled in her eyes as she dragged her feet towards the carnage. But she mustn't cry, even though she recognised some of the dead as lads from Lincluden. Men didn't cry. The Aragonese, who apparently hadn't suffered a single casualty, would think it curious. And Matthew—

She had a strange urge to shout out her glee when he appeared, Belenus following in his wake like an obedient puppy.

"Look them over. Any still alive we hold as prisoners," he shouted to the *routiers*.

The Spaniard closest to him spat, drawing an imaginary dagger across his throat. "*Matar*," he yelled. "Why we not kill?"

The rest of the Aragonese brandished daggers and took up the chant. *Matar! Matar!*

Matthew eyed her weapon, a smile tugging at the corners of his mouth.

He would likely confiscate her only means of protection. She clenched her jaw, trying to hide the terror surging in her veins.

"You will obey orders," he declared, still looking at her. "Prisoners can be of value. Dead men cannot."

He'd spoken with authority, but without shouting, without any sign he doubted his orders would be obeyed, without so much as a glance at the mercenaries.

They grumbled, but the Aragonese set about roughly herding the wounded together. Brig retreated to the rock and sank down behind it, sick at heart. If any of the captured men had recognised her as the armorer's apprentice, what would they think a Gael was doing travelling with the invaders?

# BULLIES

Matthew assessed the problem. Forcing the dozen or so prisoners to walk to Annan wasn't feasible. Two or three had significant injuries and likely wouldn't make it. The Spaniards were thirsting for blood. Confident as he was in his ability to control the mercenaries, he couldn't watch them every minute.

He'd insisted prisoners were worth more alive than dead, but he believed firmly that treating captives humanely gained more ground than cruelty. The truth of it had been borne out in every campaign he'd taken part in.

Le Cordier wouldn't be happy, but Matthew decided the best course of action was to deliver the prisoners back to Lincluden then begin the journey again on the morrow.

The Aragonese didn't take the news well. In an effort to appease them he suggested they take an hour or two's respite before beginning the march back to Lincluden. "The river is nearby. Enjoy a swim," he suggested.

He chuckled inwardly as vicious, battle-hardened brutes whooped and yelled, stripping off their armor and clothing, running for the river like carefree youths.

He glanced over at the sullen prisoners, roped together and tied to a tree. He should post a guard, but saw little need. They'd been disarmed and weren't going anywhere.

He looked around, wondering where Brig had got to. Probably still behind the outcropping. The fighting had obviously upset the lad. He sauntered over, thinking a dip in the river might revive the youth's spirits.

Brig had his back to the rock, long legs sprawled, face ashen. The dagger lay at his side, Gorrie's workmanship if Matthew wasn't mistaken. He should confiscate the weapon, but these were dangerous times when a lad might need a blade.

He startled when Matthew approached. A trickle of blood had dried on his forehead. "A stone struck you," he said, hunkering down beside the lad.

"Aye," Brig replied hoarsely. "'Tis naught. The bleeding has stopped already."

"You're lucky," Matthew said, filled with an urge to reach out and ease the pain of the wound that was rapidly turning into a livid bruise. But he thought better of it. "Scalp wounds can bleed a lot."

Brig closed his eyes. Matthew watched him, wondering what it was about this lad that drew him. He wasn't an attractive youth. The tufts of red hair made him look like a simpleton. He was tall, and working in the forge had given him muscles, but he was too willowy. And such small hands and feet.

Definitely odd, yet his face was appealing. Matthew found himself staring at the boy's mouth. His lips had fallen open. What would it be like to—

*Christ!*

He leapt to his feet, inhaling deeply to clear the fog in his brain, and the lust in his loins. Cold water was definitely what he needed. "How about a dip in the river?" he suggested.

Brig scrambled away as if Matthew had told him he was sitting on an adder's nest. "Nay, I canna swim."

In the near distance they could hear the raucous shouts of the Spaniards' horseplay.

"You don't need to swim. Just get wet. You'll feel better."

"Nay," Brig insisted, grasping for the dagger, his green eyes wary.

Water had never held any threat for Matthew. He and his brothers had enjoyed many a happy afternoon swimming in the lake near their father's manor house. He smiled at the memory. However, he had known young men who were terrified of water. He held up his palms in mock surrender. "Fine. Stay dirty. I'm not going to force you. We'll remain here for an hour then begin the trek back to Lincluden."

"We're going back?" the lad asked.

Matthew got to his feet and brushed the dust from his leggings. "We'll take the prisoners to Lincluden then set off again on the morrow. If you're not going to swim, help me take off my breastplate."

As soon as the words were out of his mouth he regretted them. His resolve had been not to touch the lad. Now he was asking him to help strip off his armor.

Brig stood, but hesitated, seemingly uncomfortable as well. Had he sensed the sinful attraction? Matthew tousled the red tufts. "Never mind. Sit. Sleep. You'll likely have an aching head soon."

He strode off , irritated with himself as he struggled to unfasten the straps of his breastplate. The sooner

Gorrie perfected the more comfortable jacket armor the better. Was was it called? A brigandine, that was it.

The realization struck him like a bolt of lightning. Brigandine—Brig. He'd thought it an unusual name, but now he understood why Gorrie had chosen it.

It was an odd name for an odd youth.

~~~

Brig slumped back against the rock, knees tucked to her chest. Matthew was right; a dull ache throbbed at her temple. However, the ache in her heart was more troubling. She'd sensed the Norman wanted to ease the pain of her wound, and was stupidly disappointed when he didn't touch her.

Sickened by the bloodshed, she'd felt a need to be held in Matthew's comforting embrace. But men didn't embrace lads. It was unmanly, and weird.

Being a lad had been easier when there was naught to it but playing games in Cruggleton's fields and helping her Da. War and death and wounded prisoners and rivers full of men cavorting around naked were harder to cope with.

Matthew must have deemed her refusal to swim peculiar. He'd looked at her in a strange way that had set her heart racing. Indeed everything about Matthew de Rowenne seemed to send her senses reeling. It was a good thing he'd decided against having her remove his armor. Her trembling hands would have raised questions in his mind.

She closed her eyes, listening to the men enjoying the river. The cool water would have felt good. Mayhap if she found a spot further upstream, away from the Spaniards, she could at least cleanse her dusty feet and dab water on the throbbing scalp wound.

She shoved the dagger back in the satchel, took a swig of water from the flask, bit off a mouthful of cheese, then looped the strap across her body and crawled like a crab towards the river. She headed upstream away from the shouting.

She was encouraged when she located a rock big enough to conceal her. She sat in the cool grass of the bank and took off her shoes, banging them together to get rid of the grit then eased her bare feet into the blessedly cold water. The river wasn't deep here but it ran swiftly. She could still hear the men, but the rock sat in the shadow of a spreading chestnut tree, so she was confident they wouldn't detect her presence. She retrieved one of the apples and bit into it, wincing at the sour taste.

She closed her eyes for a only brief moment, listening to the birds chirping in the branches above her, inhaling the scent of something she couldn't name. She swished her feet back and forth, half asleep—until hard fingers grasped her ankles.

"*Olà, niño,*" a voice taunted.

She screamed as her feet were lifted. Someone else grabbed her under the arms and she was carried into the middle of the river.

She kicked and screamed, but the Aragonese who'd stumbled upon her only laughed and tightened their grip, making what were no doubt raucous jests in their language.

She closed her eyes against their nudity, but kept on screaming and struggling. However, she had to remember they believed they were teasing a hapless

41

boy. She couldn't let them discover the truth. Despite her terror she lowered the pitch of her screams and hurled insults in Gaelic no decent woman would ever have heard.

They swung her like a sack of grain. "*Uno, dos, tres.*" On the count of three she was tossed into the river.

The water here was deeper. She floundered, flailing her arms, desperately hoping her feet would touch bottom. She struggled to the surface, gulped air then sank again, the satchel strap around her neck. She was furiously indignant that men would laugh while she drowned.

Suddenly, a strong arm clamped over her chest and drew her back to the surface. "Don't fight me," Matthew rasped. She didn't know what had become of the Aragonese and she didn't care. She went limp and allowed her hero to pull her to the shallows, fervently hoping his arm didn't dislodge the bindings.

She bent over, coughing up river water while he hurled reprimands at the sniggering Spaniards. Once she had her breath back she looked up at him.

He stood in water up to his knees. For a moment she thought she was having a vision. Before her stood the Thunder God her Norse ancestors had told of in their folklore. He was magnificent in his nakedness, the water shimmering on his muscled body, his black hair flowing like rivulets over his shoulders.

Her own body did strange things in response. She shivered. She boiled in oil. She shuddered. She shook. Her mouth fell open. Her nipples tingled. A jolt of overwhelming need stole up the inside of her thighs and into her womb.

She wanted to plunge back into the river so he could save her again.

"Leave the lad be," he shouted in Gaelic. She doubted the foreigners understood his words, but there was no mistaking his meaning, nor the menace in his voice.

But why would he come to the rescue of a youth he barely knew, the son of an armorer? A dreadful thought occurred. Mayhap he was one of those men who only liked boys.

"Are you all right, Brig?" he asked, his eyes full of concern that heightened her fear.

She scrambled to the bank, shoving the wet satchel onto her back. "Aye. I'll soon dry off. Dinna worry about me."

She hurried as fast as her wet feet would take her, reluctant to return for her shoes. She headed for the safety of the outcropping but became confused and was alarmed to find herself by the tree where the prisoners were tethered.

"Brig," one of them hissed.

Breathless, she crouched, looking back to the river to make sure no one had followed. The ache at her temple sharpened.

"Brig. 'Tis Sorley. Ye must free us."

She scurried over to the prisoners, recognizing the son of Lincluden's cook. "Sorley. What were ye thinking? Pitchforks are no match for crossbows."

He stuck out his tongue. "Some of us decided to fight for Galloway while others stayed at Lincluden and consorted with the enemy."

The barb stung. Brig didn't know how to respond.

"Ye have a dagger. I saw ye with it. Cut the rope," Sorely insisted through gritted teeth, blinking away blood dripping from a gash on his head.

Brig was conflicted. Aiding them would be a betrayal of Matthew's trust. But he was the enemy, commander of an invading army that had come to subjugate her people to the Scots. What harm in freeing Sorley? His Ma would be grateful. Matthew needn't know she was responsible.

She searched in the wet bag for the dagger, then knelt at his side and sawed through the rope binding him to the others. Despite being drenched in cold water, she was on fire. If Matthew caught her—

To her dismay, once his hands were free Sorley grabbed the weapon and set about releasing the others.

When two or three were loose, he tossed the dagger to a comrade. She scrambled to retrieve it. "Nay, ye canna all escape. How will ye get away? They'll hunt ye like animals."

Sorley grabbed her arm and yanked her to her feet. "Be a man, Brig. We'll take yon horse, ye and me."

Her heart in knots, her eyes flew to Belenus, pulling nervously at the tether that secured him to a nearby tree. It was as if the animal sensed the danger. The theft of his beloved horse would infuriate Matthew.

Sorley dragged her to Belenus, picking up a crossbow. "Get on," he shouted, levering her leg up the side of the horse's belly.

She tried to resist but he was too strong. He put his shoulder under her bottom and shoved her up. She gripped the mane as he untied the rope then leapt onto the horse's back. She clamped her hands on his shoulders as he urged the protesting horse forward. The remaining prisoners who weren't badly wounded gathered up armfuls of discarded uniforms and weapons and ran off into the wood, one of them with her dagger in his fist.

# BETRAYAL

Once the sun had more or less dried his body, Matthew picked up Brig's shoes and sauntered back to the clearing, rubbing the water from his hair. He'd deemed it better to stay away from the lad until he'd got over his upset.

The Aragonese had tired of their antics and lay around in the grass, some snoring, others laughing, sharing a jest or two. He'd given instructions for departure in an hour's time. First they would eat. The swim had given him an appetite.

He thought back to the incident with Brig. Spanish bullies, scaring the wits out of the lad. Charging to the rescue probably hadn't been necessary. He doubted the Aragonese would have allowed the lad to drown. Brig was surprisingly light for a youth of what—seventeen, eighteen? And what was the padding he wore around his chest? Mayhap some sort of protection Gorrie had fashioned. Sensible idea really for a father worried about his son's survival.

Anyone would think from the way Brig had gawked at him after the rescue that the lad had never seen a naked man before. What was more perplexing was the lunatic urge that had seized him to strut like a rooster under the youth's startled gaze.

He reached the clearing and realized Belenus was gone. His roar of denial brought the Spaniards hurrying to his side.

"The captives have escaped," he shouted through gritted teeth.

Panic seized him. Brig!

He ran to the outcropping expecting to see the lad cowering there. The truth hit him like a blow to the belly.

*He has betrayed me.*

The peculiar boy who drew him like a lodestone had freed the prisoners and stolen his horse. He stared at the rock, teetering on the precipice of furious despair, feeling somehow he had lost more than his horse—and most of his brigade's clothing.

Then it came to him he still held Brig's shoes in his grip.

The youth had fled barefoot. Only a fool would—

A spark of hope flickered in his breast. Perhaps Brig hadn't gone willingly. He'd been in a state of panic when he'd left the river. Mayhap one of the prisoners had got loose and—

This fiasco was his responsibility. Leaving captives unattended was folly. He'd go after them, hunt them down and if he found Brig was guilty of treason, he'd see him hung.

He walked back to the clearing. The sight of the Aragonese squabbling over what remained of the uniforms irritated him further.

He barked curt orders, organizing the melee. To his relief one of the Aragonese came forward with his leggings and breastplate. But his boots were nowhere to be found.

The walk back to Lincluden would be a complete humiliation. Some of his soldiers were still in a state of undress, but only four crossbows had been taken. At least they'd have a chance if the escaped prisoners attacked again.

"*Los otros cautivos?*" a soldier asked, pointing to the badly wounded Gaels.

"Leave them," Matthew responded without a glance at the four wretches. "They weren't able to flee when they had the chance. We can't burden ourselves with them now."

The Aragonese fell in behind him as they began the trek back to Lincluden. It was too hot to wear his breastplate, so he carried it, swearing vengeance on the boy he'd trusted.

The loss of Belenus was one thing. His heart cleaved in two when it came to him his cloak was in his saddlebag, along with the treasured brooch. The heirloom might carry a tainted legacy, but it was his legacy, the only thing of true value he possessed. He'd get it back no matter what it took.

~~~

Brig clung to Sorley as he drove the horse over the moor. Trotting leisurely behind Matthew had been pleasant. Galloping at full tilt over uncertain terrain was terrifying. Sorley had slung the crossbow over one shoulder and the lethal weapon dug into the flesh of her arm. She shivered in the wet clothing, praying the soaking wet bindings still concealed her breasts. It felt like they'd loosened.

She tried to think how a youth would react. What to

say to Sorley? He'd surely see the terror on her face when they finally stopped.

He seemed to be heading somewhat in the direction of Lincluden, and yet he wasn't. She plucked up her courage. "Where are we going?" she yelled in his ear.

"Twelve Apostles," he shouted over his shoulder.

She was none the wiser until he slowed Belenus. In the near distance loomed a circle of stones. "Gatherin' place for our people for hundreds of years," he rasped. "Ye won't ha known o' it, coming from Cruggleton."

"Nay," she replied, keeping her voice low. "Twelve Apostles. I suppose there are twelve stones."

He didn't reply as they rode into the field of monoliths. Even in daylight the place made Brig's skin crawl. Most were upright, all twice her height. A few lay on their sides, one or two at least as long as three men lying head to toe.

"How did they get here?" she asked, nervous that lads didn't ask such questions.

Sorley reined Belenus to a halt. "Nobody knows. Some say 'twas the work of the Disciples. Most believe the Druids erected 'em thousands o' years ago."

He slid from the horse and she followed his lead. "But for what purpose?" she asked, again wondering if her curiosity would arouse his suspicions.

However, he seemed more than ready to show off his knowledge. "They say 'twas to do with the solstice, others think it was a temple for making sacrifices to the gods."

Brig shuddered, despite the heat of the afternoon.

She thought of Matthew, forced to walk back to Lincluden. How furious he must be. He would know by now she'd betrayed him.

Sorley pointed west. "There's a smaller circle a few miles away in that direction where the others are camped, and one more a mile or so to the east."

*The others?*

It occurred to Brig that most of the folk at Lincluden likely knew of these circles. It wouldn't take Matthew and Le Cordier long to ferret out information about where the fugitives might have headed. "He'll come after us, ye ken," she said, stroking Belenus's nose. "If only for the horse."

Sorley shrugged and began rummaging through the leather bag hanging from the saddle. He pulled out a cloak. Her knees threatened to buckle when she caught sight of the brooch with the red glass.

"Look at this," Sorley exclaimed. He unfastened the pin and held it up to the sunlight. "'Tis a treasure we've found." He squinted. "Summat engraved on it. Latin I think."

"I canna read," she said sadly, sure in her heart Matthew valued this keepsake possibly more than his horse. She'd never seen him without it.

Sorley pinned it to his shirt. It looked like a jewel stuck into a turd. He strutted like a rooster, one hand on his hip, the crossbow still on his shoulder. "Behold the Lord of Galloway," he crowed.

Blurting out her fears wouldn't be manly. She opted for sarcasm. "Ye'll be a dead lord when the Norman catches up to ye. And what's the point of a crossbow with no bolts? Some leader ye are."

The smile left Sorley's face. "Better than a coward like ye, Brig Lordsmith. Dinna fash about crossbow bolts. Easy to steal they are. 'Twas the bows we were lacking."

She decided to ignore the slur. A suspicion was growing the crossbows had been the reason for the ill-fated attack. Men had been deliberately sacrificed for the stolen weapons. "And what if the others dinna make it here? We had a horse. They're on foot, some of them wounded."

"That's why ye'll stay here and I'll go back," he said.

She could have retorted that such a plan was foolhardy, but confused thoughts assailed her. On the one hand she'd be glad to be rid of Sorley's unpleasant company. On the other the prospect of being left alone in the field of standing stones was dreadful, especially once night fell. Her garments were still damp, and well, the place was eerie.

She gambled. "At least leave me the cloak," she insisted with as much bravado as she could muster. "And ye canna be serious about letting the others see yon brooch. They'll slit yer throat fer it."

He hesitated, then to her immense relief, unpinned the jewel and thrust it and the cloak at her. "Ye'd better still be here when I return," he said.

# TWELVE APOSTLES

Brig repinned the brooch onto Matthew's cloak, then ran her finger over the symbols engraved into the glass, filled with a strange premonition it was important to know what the words meant. But such a notion was hopeless. Latin, Sorley had said. She couldn't even read Gaelic.

She studied the lettering, suddenly noticing the symbols were the same whichever way you looked at them. Backwards and forwards, they were the same. Curious. It strengthened her belief Matthew would hunt down the traitors who'd stolen his horse and his unusual keepsake.

Shivering, she folded the garment carefully and left it on a rock. For close to what she guessed was an hour she wandered from stone to stone, clambering up on each of the lower ones to scan the horizon. Moorland greeted the eye as far as she could see in every direction, but she really had no notion which way to go. Darkness would descend soon and she'd no wish to be out on the moor alone at night. Nor did she want to stumble into the *others*, whoever they were, camped at the neighboring circle. She suspected the missing men from Lincluden lurked there in anticipation of Gilbride's return. It was possible they roamed the moor at night, hunting mayhap. Or perhaps there were wolves about.

She returned to the big rock where she'd left the cloak. It occurred to her the brooch might prove to be a valuable bargaining piece, and she didn't want Sorley to have it. She glanced across the field to the tallest stone. Part of its base seemed to hang over nothingness. She ran to it and nervously inched her hand underneath. Just enough space. A natural hiding place. She tore a strip of linen off the bottom of her shirt, traced a fingertip over the elaborate knobs and circles worked into the brooch, wrapped the treasure and secreted it beneath the overhang.

Her bare feet were cut and freezing. The wind had picked up. She retrieved the cloak from the flat rock and furled it around her shoulders. She threw out the sodden bread, but forced herself to eat the waterlogged cheese and the last sour apple. As darkness fell she huddled against the rock and tented the cloak over her, wrapping the hem around her feet. She inhaled the scent of Matthew de Rowenne that lingered in the wool, wishing he was there to spirit her away. She'd always believed she could take care of herself, but that was before the Norman had awakened feelings and emotions she'd never known. Being a lad had lost its appeal. The protection of a strong man was what she needed. Matthew de Rowenne was the one she wanted. But he already hated her. When he discovered she was a girl, and there was no escaping that now, he would despise her even more. And what business did a smith's daughter have dreaming of a nobleman.

She was exhausted but didn't dare sleep. Without a

weapon she had no means of defence. If man or beast stalked her, flight would be the only chance of survival.

She watched the moon rise, dozing fitfully until she heard someone calling her name.

It was Sorley, but she hadn't heard Belenus.

She thought of staying hidden behind the rock, but he'd find her eventually. "O'er here," she shouted.

He and another youth limped out of the darkness. Sorley stumbled to his knees beside her. "*Fyking* 'orse!" he rasped. He rolled over onto his back, breathing heavily.

She couldn't make out the other lad's face, but the moonlight glinted off a dagger tucked into his belt—her dagger. She edged away from them. "What happened?"

"Threw us off," Sorley whined, rubbing his hip.

An urge to giggle seized her, but she thought better of it.

"Middle o' nowhere. Had to walk back. Cudda broke me leg. Gimme the cloak, I'm freezing."

Brig wasn't done with being a lad yet. "Nay. Me clothes are still damp. I'll catch me death if I give ye the cloak. 'Tis mine now. I was well accepted by the Englishman. Good way to spy on the invaders if ye'd thought about it afore draggin' me off. Ye were too busy accusin' me o' being a coward."

"A spy?" he whispered, his teeth chattering.

The other youth loomed over her, one hand resting against the rock.

She had no choice but to continue with the deception. "Aye, Sorley, ye great mawp. If ye'd think on it, we canna win this fight with pitchforks and a few stolen crossbows. We need to be canny, to watch and wait for the right chances."

She hoped her bravado was convincing.

Sorley was silent for a long while before he bent close to her ear and whispered, "Where's the jewel?"

She'd hoped the darkness had hidden the fact the brooch wasn't pinned to the cloak, and he evidently didn't want the other lad to know of it. His greed had pushed him to ask. She took a deep breath and whispered back, "I hid it where ye'll ne'er find it. 'Tis my assurance ye'll no harm me."

It was a mistake.

"Harm ye?" he shouted, his sour breath invading her nostrils. "Ye sound like a girl. 'Course, ye always did."

Her throat constricted. Had he guessed?

The other boy drew the dagger. "Always wondered what Brig Lordsmith had 'twixt his legs."

She recognised his gravelly voice now. Hamish, the Cruggleton bully she'd avoided. Nervously she looked up at him. His eyes glowed in the dark like some feral beast. If he didn't know her secret, he suspected. She tried to get to her feet, but Sorley grasped her wrists and held her down. "Let's find out," he cried.

Hamish dropped to his knees, put the dagger between his teeth and ripped open the front of her shirt from bottom to top. He took the dagger out of his mouth. "What's this?" he asked, trailing the point of the blade the length of the bindings.

There was no one to aid her as she kicked and struggled, screaming at the top of her lungs.

~~~

Matthew heard a woman's strident screaming. Not too far away standing stones loomed like black giants against the moonlit sky. Mayhap it was an ancient druid circle where the fugitives might have gathered. Was some sort of sacrifice going on? He'd previously discredited reports of such rituals carried out by barbarians in the untamed regions north of Cumbria.

He motioned the *routiers* on foot behind him to halt and lower their torches.

He patted Belenus. "Good lad," he said.

The beast tossed his head.

What a horse! Matthew had feared his lacerated feet wouldn't carry him another step when the trusty animal had appeared on the castle road, having evidently rid himself of his riders. Even the Spaniards had cheered when Belenus bucked and pranced, lapping up the praise.

Matthew had ridden ahead to Lincluden, ignored the sniggers of the men on watch, avoided Le Cordier who was reportedly busy with a more pressing matter, found another pair of boots and fresh clothing, put on his breastplate and been ready to ride out all within the space of an hour.

The half dressed and weary Aragonese were trickling into Lincluden by the time he'd picked out a handful of Brabanters to accompany him. No one was going to steal Matthew de Rowenne's horse and clothing and make a complete fool of him—especially not the son of a blacksmith.

Belenus would lead the way to the enemy—to Brig.

The screams were unexpected, but a woman was obviously in dire distress. No choice but to urge his horse forward.

He galloped into what turned out to be a circle of

standing stones spread out over a field. He reined to a halt, listening. There seemed to be a scuffle going on beside one of the fallen rocks. He drew his sword and charged, yelling a guttural war cry.

Two or three people burst forth, running in different directions. It would take a few minutes for the mercenaries to arrive. He stopped, uncertain which fugitive to follow, until the moonlight fell on a red cloak. His cloak. He sheathed his weapon, dismounted and ran after the fleeing figure.

It was definitely Brig. It would give him no pleasure to give the lad the beating of his life, but it had to be done.

The youth darted in and out of the stones, following what seemed to be a well worn path, the cloak billowing out behind him. Matthew considered cutting across the field to head him off, but keeping to the circular path was probably a better idea. The lad was tiring, he could tell.

Matthew's shredded feet pained him. He wished he'd taken the time to pull on hose. Now he'd have blisters on top of everything else. Enough of this running around in circles in the middle of the night.

The notion almost brought him to his knees.

*In girum imus nocte.*

But that was only half the cursed motto. He glanced over to where the Brabanters had appeared, flaming torches held high. They were on a collision course with Brig. The mercenaries wouldn't hesitate to thrust the torches at the lad. He couldn't let him be burned to death. A memory of his mother's ghastly demise and his father's anguish loomed in the giant shadows cast by the standing stones. He forced himself to run faster, ignoring the sharp pain stabbing his ribs. Brig slowed to catch his breath. Matthew leapt on him and they tumbled to the ground.

He took in great gulps of air, filled with conflicting emotions. He'd taken a liking to this lad, odd as he was, been drawn to him in sinful ways no warrior wanted to admit to. Now the boy's sobs tore at his confused heart. But treachery had to be punished.

"Follow the others," he yelled to the mercenaries, satisfied he'd captured his quarry.

He straddled Brig's thighs, forced the panting youth over onto his back, and clenched his fist.

The lad raised his hands to protect his face, but Matthew's gut knotted at the sight of two perfect female breasts glowing like silver orbs in the moonlight. Nestled in shredded bindings, they rose and fell with each shuddering sob.

His lungs refused to work. His mind taunted that he'd been a fool, taken in by a chit of a girl. But his heart rejoiced. His body had known she was a female all along. An urge to lick her nipples and suckle hard had him trembling like a leaf. He welcomed the intensely pleasurable erection her body aroused.

"Brigandine," he rasped, gathering his cloak to cover her nudity. He wasn't sure if his trembling knees would sustain him as he scooped her up and got to his feet.

She snaked her arms around his neck and rested her head on his shoulder. "Forgive me, Matthew," she murmured. "Your brooch is safe."

It humbled him. He kissed the red tufts he'd once deemed ugly, relishing their silkiness on his lips. She'd been brutally attacked yet her concern was for his pin. He'd worried about a ritual sacrifice. Now he understood her attackers had intended to spill virgin blood. A quick glance at her clothing seemed to indicate they hadn't achieved their goal, but his heart leapt into his throat—he'd almost arrived too late. There was no doubt in his mind she was an innocent, and he burned to be the one to take this woman's maidenhead.

The notion stunned him. She was the daughter of a smith. When Henry knighted him and granted an estate he couldn't take a tradesman's daughter to wife, a girl who'd been an armorer's apprentice. The irony of it. He'd spent his adult life trying to distance himself from such humble ancestors.

In any case, he'd sworn never to wed. Watching his father die of grief and guilt had been enough to dissuade him from marriage. It would tear him apart if Brigandine died a horrible death because of him.

*Et consumimur igni.*

*We are consumed by fire.*

"Show me where it is," he rasped, wishing he had the courage to leave the cursed heirloom where it lay hidden.

# THE CAMPFIRE

Brigandine stared into the flames of the hearty fire the Brabanters had lit in the shelter of the tallest stone. She sat in Matthew's lap. He'd draped his cloak over his shoulders and cocooned her inside it, his arms around her. The fire had stopped her teeth chattering; being held against his body engulfed her in heat. Yet she shivered inwardly, dreading what might happen now he knew the truth.

He wasn't the only one who'd made startling discoveries this night. Brig the boy had become Brigandine the woman. Her body's eager acceptance of her femininity had been a shock.

She'd retrieved Matthew's brooch. It lay in her palm. He seemed reluctant to take it from her. They'd exchanged few words since the rescue. The mercenaries kept watch around the outer edges of the circle. Sorley and Hamish had eluded them, and she'd no intention of telling Matthew about the other stone circle nearby.

She touched the red glass. "'Tis beautiful," she whispered, desperate to break the silence.

He only grunted in reply, nuzzling her ear.

She traced a fingertip over the inscription, shoving aside the silly female question that nagged. He was a man. He'd seen her breasts. His surprise had been evident, but did he find them appealing? She'd overheard enough bawdy talk among the youth of Cruggleton Castle to know the hard bulge beneath her bottom said he did.

Instead she said, "Tell me what it means."

The smoke drifted towards them as the wind shifted. She coughed, rubbing her eyes. He pressed her head to his chest and buried his face in her hair. She would never smell woodsmoke again without thinking of him and of this night.

She harbored no illusions. He was an ambitious nobleman, a warrior, she was a—

What was she now?

When the wind changed again, he took the brooch and read the inscription. *"In girum imus nocte et consumimur igni."*

The deep richness of his voice echoed up her spine. He paused but she sensed he would explain the meaning.

"It's a palindrome," he said. "Reads the same in both directions."

She felt proud she'd been right.

"In Latin it's humorous, but the humor is lost in your language and mine. *We run around in circles at night and are consumed by fire.*"

She gasped. "The first part came true tonight. We ran round in circles."

He remained silent.

"How old is the brooch?" she asked, uncertain why she needed to know more about this piece of jewellery.

"Hundreds of years," he replied, but she sensed no enthusiasm in his voice. "It was handed down from an ancestor who was a sword-smith."

She laughed. "A sword-smith? Like my father?"

She thought it humorous, but his clenched jaw indicated he didn't. She should have kept silent but instead—

"What does it mean *consumed by fire*?"

He shrugged. "Who knows. Best we get some sleep. The morrow will be a difficult day."

He pinned the brooch onto his cloak and stretched down in the shelter of the rock, tucking her back into his chest, his arm clamped around her. She fell asleep determined to savor this chance to be consumed by the heat of his body. It was unlikely it would ever happen again.

This was the calm before the storm.

~~~

Either Matthew's feet had swollen or his boots had shrunk. He recalled woefully that this particular pair had always been snug. The cuts on the soles of his feet prickled as if he'd walked on hot coals. He considered easing the boots off, but suspected they'd be hard to remove and didn't want to wake Brigandine.

The embers of the fire still glowed, warming them within the enchanted circle. This night she was safe in his arms. On the morrow—

His head swam with conflicting emotions. What was it about this woman that attracted him? He chuckled inwardly. Attraction was too weak a word for what he felt. The urge to mate with her was overwhelming, yet he had no wish to use her as his mistress, and the fullness at his groin was pleasantly reassuring that his yearning was natural.

But natural or not, there was no future for them. On the morrow the spell would be broken. They'd return to Lincluden where she and her father would no doubt face censure. Le Cordier might not deem the masquerade of any importance, but the castle folk would make the pair suffer for it. If Gorrie lost his livelihood, he and his daughter would be destitute.

Matthew resolved to do all in his power to ensure Gorrie remained as armorer to the English army. But Brigandine could no longer be his apprentice—could she?

He'd a feeling she loved the work. If she wanted to carry on he'd support her.

Marrying Brig might solve many of the problems that lay ahead. He fingered the brooch as a reminder of why that would never be possible.

He had to keep his eye on the prize; land, a knighthood. Those were the important things.

She turned in her sleep and her hand settled on his neck. Savoring the innocent intimacy of her gesture, he studied her lovely face in the firelight. How had he not realized? She was stunningly beautiful, even with the strange hair and the bruise on her temple. Though her hands were calloused, they were dainty and feminine. But she could never be his and his heart ached with the bitter truth of it.

# KEEPING THE SECRET

The noisy shouts of the Brabanters woke Matthew as dawn broke. He wasn't alarmed. The mercenaries never did anything quietly. But he didn't want them to discover Brig in his arms, having decided during the night that maintaining her disguise was the safest plan for the moment

Reluctantly, he gently shook her awake. She blinked open her eyes and gazed at him. What he saw in those green depths was humbling. She trusted him. Perhaps she had feelings for him too, but that would complicate matters further. "We must continue your masquerade," he rasped, removing his cloak and wrapping it tightly around her. The backs of his hands brushed against her breasts. Despite his determination to discourage any relationship between them, he had to tell her. "You are the most beautiful woman I've ever set eyes on, Brigandine."

There was just enough light to reveal her blush. She said nothing in reply, but her eyes smiled.

He fastened the cloak with his pin, somehow knowing he could trust her with it. "Only I know of your sex," he said. "We must keep it that way."

She averted her gaze. "Sorley and Hamish know," she murmured.

He got to his feet, took her hand and pulled her up. "It won't take long to track them. They will probably lead us to other rebels."

She eyed him curiously. He kept forgetting she was a Gael who'd betrayed him once already.

"I didn't want to betray you," she said, as if she recognised his fear. "I was angry and upset and only meant to free Sorley. He stole my dagger and freed the others and forced me to go with him when he took Belenus. I knew you would be furious about your horse."

It pleased him that she cared. "I want to fold you in my arms, Brigandine and kiss you, but I fear the mercenaries might see us and wonder." He grinned. "It's strange, I thought Brig an ugly name, now I can't stop saying Brigandine."

Belenus whinnied nearby. "He knows it's time to go."

She followed him to his horse and watched him mount. He smiled weakly, his hand held out. "I'd prefer to sit you on my lap, but again—"

She nodded, accepted his hand and mounted behind him. "I understand," she said. "I thank ye. My Da will be grateful."

It occurred to him she wouldn't be in this precarious position were it not for her father, but he said nothing in reply. He might have done the same in Gorrie's place. He shook away the notion. If he had a daughter —

Irritated with himself, he urged Belenus forward. There would be no daughters, no sons either if he never married. Despite his resolve, the notion saddened him.

He relished the warmth of Brigandine's body pressed

to his back, especially now he'd seen her glorious breasts. Her thighs hugged his arse. Strong thighs, made to wrap around a man's hips.

His shaft reacted predictably to the arousing vision that played behind his eyes. "Lincluden. March," he yelled gruffly to the Brabanters, hoping to take his mind off the woman whose heat already had him sweating. They fell into formation behind him.

~~~

Brigandine was lazily enjoying the leisurely ride back to Lincluden. No matter what happened, Matthew de Rowenne deemed her the most beautiful woman he'd ever set eyes on. She found herself thrusting out the breasts she'd been careful to hide. The sensation wrought by her nipples rubbing against his back through the fabric of his cloak was indescribable. It made her want. What she wanted she wasn't sure but it certainly involved Matthew.

As they came within sight of the castle he reined to an abrupt halt, gritting out something in his own language she suspected was an oath. "What's wrong?"

"Atop the flag pole," he replied flatly. "King William's standard."

She squinted up at the pennant fluttering in the early morning breeze. "How do ye know?"

"The red lion. That's his symbol. That's why he's called William the Lion. Believe me it has naught to do with his prowess."

The hint of humor in his voice intrigued her. "Ye sound like ye know him."

"I unhorsed him at the Battle of Alnwick."

Pride surged through her veins. The man she loved

had unhorsed a king!

Wait! Loving Matthew was impossible.

"Then I escorted him to Normandie. In chains."

This was troubling news that plummeted like a lead ball to the pit of her belly. "He'll nay be happy to see ye, then," she murmured.

"That's what I'm afraid of," he replied, setting Belenus in motion again.

They trotted into the bailey and dismounted. A stable boy ran to take the reins, and one of the Spanish soldiers hurried towards them. She edged closer to Matthew, fairly sure this was one of the bullies who'd dunked her in the river. "*Commandante*," he said with a crisp bow before rattling off some message in his own language. He bowed again then stood to attention.

She hadn't understood a word, but relief showed on Matthew's face. "Le Cordier is with the king in the Hall," he explained. "He knows nothing of what happened on the way to Annan, only that we were attacked. The Aragonese told him I had gone in search of the rebels."

She was awed that Matthew commanded the respect of the rough Spaniards. They'd protected him.

To her surprise he patted her bottom. "Hie away to the forge," he said with a smile. "Don't tell your Da I know the truth. Tell no one."

Heart racing, she nodded, unpinning the brooch. He put a hand over hers. Its reassuring warmth traveled from her hand up her spine and into her womb. "Leave it on until you can replace the bindings. Act quickly. I'll come for the cloak."

He winked. "I must go," he rasped. "A king awaits."

It was exhilarating. A man, winking at her, as if they shared a secret. Which they did! And he was trusting her with his jewel.

"Go with God," she whispered, watching him stride off with the Spaniard in his wake. When he disappeared into the castle keep, she dashed off to the forge.

# CADHA

Matthew found the King and Le Cordier in the Hall. William dwarfed the Lord's Chair, drumming the fat fingers of one hand on the elaborately carved arm. Matthew bent the knee, but his homage was prompted by custom not respect, and he sensed King William the Lion knew it. "Your Majesty," he gushed in Norman French.

Le Cordier bristled. "His Majesty has been waiting."

Matthew widened his eyes. "I apologise, Your Majesty, I was abroad pursuing men who have rebelled against your rule. Had I known—"

William waved a lazy hand. "You've arrived at last, de Rowenne, and I am less than pleased my cousin chose you for this campaign."

Matthew bowed in acknowledgement, but refrained from remarking that was exactly the reason Henry had sent him. "I regret my presence displeases you, Your Majesty. I am a humble soldier and I do my duty when it is asked of me."

Le Cordier cleared his throat. "If I may speak—"

"Nay, you may not," William interjected, "because you are about to tell me de Rowenne is a dependable soldier who proved his worth in the last Scottish expedition—the one Henry sent into my country while

69

I was his *guest* in Normandie."

The interview wasn't going well. Matthew deemed it advisable to say nothing.

"Concerning the location of my castle in Galloway," William asked unexpectedly, "what say you, de Rowenne? The Nith or the Annan?"

Matthew had no way of knowing what had passed between the King and Le Cordier, but was firmly convinced as to where the fortification should be built. "South of here, Sire, on the Nith."

He sensed his *capitaine's* agitation.

William stroked his red beard. "Agreed," he declared after several minutes of silence. "Now, on another matter. Ranulf de Glanville has charged me with finding a bride for you."

Matthew had a strange feeling Le Cordier was stifling a smile behind his twitching lips. That didn't augur well. The familiar desperation rose again in his throat, but William would quickly quell his objections and the reasons for them. But he was completely unprepared for what the king said next.

"I have chosen Lady Cadha MacFergus."

The name was vaguely familiar. "MacFergus?" he asked.

"Aye," William replied with a broad grin. "Daughter of Gilbride, so called Lord of Galloway."

The ground shifted beneath Matthew's feet. He determined to keep the consternation out of his voice. "Surely, Your Majesty, MacFergus will not allow his daughter to wed a lowly soldier?"

The king fixed his gaze on Matthew. "Don't concern yourself with that. Cadha is his sixth daughter. He has already consigned her to a nunnery. Too many daughters, too many dowries."

More retaliation. Matthew was being forced to wed a woman who would bring nothing to the marriage. He was a worm wriggling on a fish hook. "But if she has taken vows—"

William steepled his fingers, obviously enjoying Matthew's discomfort. "Nay, just a novice. We got her out just in time."

"Out?" he parroted.

"From Lincluden Abbey," Le Cordier supplied. "I escorted her here yesterday."

This explained the important matter that had preoccupied his *capitaine*. His bride-to-be was in Lincluden Castle; and why did Le Cordier find the turn of events so amusing?

The king had no way of knowing he'd cursed Cadha MacFergus to a fiery death, and it was likely he wouldn't care if he did. But he knew full well he'd brought Gilbride's wrath down on Matthew's head. The Lord of Galloway would take the abduction and unsanctioned marriage of his daughter as a personal insult.

Only King Henry could prevent this marriage now, and he had returned to Normandie before Matthew's departure for Carlisle.

He was a dead man.

~~~

Brig's Da had pestered her for hours about the attack until she'd snapped back that she was sworn to secrecy. Deceiving her father was wrong, but she'd given

Matthew her word. Gorrie sulked, pounding the ingot he'd been working on for days, apparently annoyed he knew as little as anyone else in the castle. The Aragonese had closed ranks.

"Well, we had our own excitement here yesterday," he finally said. "King William and Le Cordier abducted Gilbride's daughter from the Abbey."

"Cadha?" Brig asked, remembering the shy girl she'd known in Cruggleton. "Why would they do that? It's been her lifelong wish to give herself to God. She has a true vocation."

"Aye, well," Gorrie replied, "rumor has it she's to wed the Norman."

Brig understood now what *consumed by fire* meant. The burning pain of jealous disbelief scorched her heart. "De Rowenne?"

"Aye, but ye can ask him. Here he comes now, no doubt for his cloak," her father remarked.

She watched as Matthew walked slowly towards her, his face ashen, and she knew it was true. Her heart was broken, her shoes nailed to the stone floor, but she had to go to him.

She hastily retrieved the folded cloak she'd made ready in anticipation of his visit, and ran to him. They weren't the only people in the field, but at least her father was too far away to overhear. She thrust the cloak at the man who preoccupied her every waking and sleeping moment, averting her eyes from the red glass. "I hear ye're to be wed," she said brightly.

He accepted the cloak, one brow arched. "News travels fast," he quipped with a smile that held no humor.

Brigandine swallowed the knot in her throat. "I wish ye the best. Cadha is a sweet lass."

"You know her?" he asked with wide eyed surprise.

"Aye. We grew up together in Cruggleton, though of course she was a nobleman's daughter and I was the smith's apprentice."

Matthew clenched his jaw and looked to the sky.

Brig remembered resting her hand on that long neck. The memory filled her with longing. She resolved to speak of other things. "But I always thought Cadha would become a religious."

He narrowed his eyes and frowned. "Because she's Gilbride's sixth daughter?"

"Nay, because she has a true calling."

His gaze darkened. "She doesn't want to marry?"

"She aspires to be the bride of Christ."

Matthew studied his feet. She glanced around. People were becoming curious. She was at a loss. "But she'll be a faithful wife."

He looked up sharply. "I don't want a wife."

His anger took her aback. The news about Cadha had destroyed any silly notions about her and Matthew. Now he was trampling them in the dirt. "I'm sorry. I thought most men sought to wed."

He furled the cloak around his shoulders, his jaw clenched. He unpinned the clasp of the brooch, but held it out, his eyes locked on hers. "This is the reason I will never marry. You asked what *consumed by fire* meant. This heirloom has been handed down through my family for generations, always to the second son. The last three wives of those men all died by fire, including my mother. I'll not wish that on any woman, especially one I love."

Brig swayed like a sapling in the wind, wishing she could throw herself at him, tell him he was wrong. Fire was already consuming her. He'd never met Cadha. If he loved a woman, it could only be—

"Ye love me?" she ventured in a hoarse voice she barely recognised.

He pinned the brooch back on the cloak then looked back into her eyes. "I am not master of my own destiny, Brigandine Lordsmith. If I was—"

He turned and strode way abruptly before she had a chance to tell him she would risk anything to spend her life with him, no matter how short that life, nor how painful the end of it.

# FLIGHT

Brig saw Matthew only occasionally over the course of the next few days. He never stopped on his way by the forge, never looked her way. Preparations were in hand for construction to begin on a new castle fortification south of Lincluden at Dumfries. She accepted he must be preoccupied with his responsibilities on that front, but it hurt nonetheless to see him so obviously unhappy, his jaw clenched, face grim.

With her female emotions in turmoil, playing the role of a lad was becoming nigh on intolerable, but her father needed her as the workload increased in the smithy.

Rumor had it Matthew had been introduced to his betrothed. She wondered what he thought of Cadha. She hadn't mentioned the lazy eye and slurred speech, but he must know of the girl's physical shortcomings by now. It was reported she'd left the interview in tears, stammering her objections.

The pounding of her Da's sledgehammer had never bothered Brig, but now every blow rang in her head. She absent-mindedly pressed her fingertips to the bruise at her temple. It had almost disappeared, but the memory of Matthew's concern brought her close to tears. That was the trouble with being a girl. She seemed to be constantly teetering on the verge of tears.

She wept with relief when it was whispered the men hiding at the druid circle had eluded the mercenaries who'd gone to ferret them out. That meant Sorley and Hamish were probably still alive, but it gave renewed hope for Gilbride's triumphant return, and an ousting of the Scots. She worried though that the arrival of Scottish troops with King William had crammed Lincluden to the rafters with armed men. Gilbride would need to lay siege with a huge army. But if the English were routed, Matthew might be killed or injured.

At night she cried for Cadha, denied her vocation, a hostage. She felt sorry for the girl, but hated her at the same time. She was to be Matthew's wife. Brig resented the thought of him even touching Gilbride's daughter.

She sobbed into her bed linens, longing for Matthew. He needed a strong woman, a fiery woman. A protector. A Brigandine. But he believed himself cursed.

Her misery was compounded daily by Le Cordier who strutted around, looking pleased with himself. She cringed whenever he came near the smithy, thrown off balance by the lecherous way he looked at her. Either he'd found out she was a girl, or he was one of those men who—

"Bellows, Brig," her Da shouted. "By the saints, stop yer daydreamin'."

Jolted from her thoughts, she hastily pumped the lever she'd been leaning on, bringing life to the fire.

Things had to change. There was no going back to being a lad. She resolved to do everything in her power to save Matthew from a disastrous marriage and the enslavement of his curse.

~~~

It wasn't difficult to find the location of Cadha's chamber. Lincluden was a small castle, much of it too dilapidated to be habitable. However, the maid who told Brig where it was also mentioned the two-man guard posted at the door.

Nothing for it but to enter from outside. Brig was confident she was skinny enough to fit through the narrow window, even wearing one of her father's brigandine jackets. She hoped Cadha hadn't grown any fatter.

Though not on the ground floor, the chamber's window was fortuitously located next to a buttress. She crawled up the sloping wall like a crab, dismayed that the top seemed a lot higher than she'd thought. She'd brought along one of her father's smaller swords, just in case, but it was proving to be a hindrance. It scraped on the stone, and she almost tripped over it more than once. The belt of the scabbard was far too big, despite the extra holes she'd dug into the leather with an awl and the padding provided by the brigandine.

When she reached the more gently sloped top she rested on all fours, trying to catch her breath.

She was about to tap on the window when a patrol of sentries went by, talking loudly in Spanish. In the event they did look up, she was confident the clouds obscuring the moon would be enough to conceal her. The version of the brigandine she'd borrowed had thin plates of armor on the outside and if she survived this escapade she resolved to mention to her father that wasn't necessarily appropriate for clandestine nighttime sorties.

Cadha came to the window after three taps, the third more insistent than the first two. Brig motioned for her to open the window. She seemed hesitant at first, but her peculiar eyes widened in recognition and she complied. Brig crawled into the chamber and pressed a forefinger to her lips.

"You're the armorer's s-s-son," Cadha whispered.

"Aye," Brig replied. "I've come to help ye escape."

Cadha made the sign of her Savior across her body. "G-g-god b-b-bless you, for He has s-s-surely sent you to m-m-y aid."

Brig felt like a fraud. Was she doing this for Cadha's sake or for her own? No time to worry about that. The Day of Judgement would come soon enough. "We'll have to escape through the window," she whispered.

"Th-th-then wh-wh-what?" Cadha asked.

Brig was reluctant to admit she hadn't really thought about what came next. "We'll need a horse."

Cadha nodded. She had no way of knowing Brig had never ridden a horse, except behind Matthew. But there was one mount she might be able to control. She'd take Belenus and have him back in the stables by dawn. Matthew would never know. "We'll ride to the Abbey and ye'll be safe."

Cadha shook her head. "N-n-not unless I pr-pr-pr-profess my f-f-final v-v-vows."

This was true. King William had paid no mind to the sanctity of the Abbey, but forcing a nun to break her vows would consign him to Hell. "We'll get the priest, from the village," she declared, fearing the bad-tempered Father Ailig wouldn't be happy about being awakened in the middle of the night.

"No n-n-need," Cadha replied. "B-b-bishop M-m-m-mort-t-timer is on r-r-r-etr-r-r-eat at the A-a-a-abbey."

To Brig's further relief, the would-be nun hoisted the hem of her postulant's robe and raised her knee to the sill of the window.

"Ye'll have to crawl onto the top of the buttress wall," Brig explained, "then go down backwards, like a crab."

Cadha looked at her as if she'd spoken in Greek, but then smiled and said, "B-b-best not to look d-d-down, I s-s-suppose."

Brig worried about the lazy eye. Did the girl have any balance? "Aye, and stay still if sentries pass by."

Heart-stopping minutes later they were running for the stables. The sword felt strange bouncing on Brig's hip, and she feared Cadha's white robes would stand out like a bonfire if the clouds rolled on. Thanks be to the saints it was a new moon.

They heard the snores of the stable guard before they got to the door. They tiptoed past him and easily found Belenus. The horse nickered softly in recognition, but there was no saddle, and Brig didn't know how to put one on. "We'll have to ride bareback," she rasped.

To her surprise, Cadha seized a saddle from the partition wall and hefted it across the horse's back. It seemed to take her only a few seconds to saddle and bridle the animal. Belenus stood stock still. Brig gawked in amazement when Cadha straddled the beast and held out her hand. "R-r-ridden s-s-since I was a ch-ch-child," she said with a smile.

Of course. This girl was the daughter of a nobleman. Brig took her hand and scrambled up.

"G-g-god is w-w-with us," Cadha whispered as they rode slowly out of the stables and on to the path to the Abbey.

Brig's heart filled with hope. Mayhap Cadha was right.

~~~

From the shadows Matthew watched Brig and Cadha make their escape. A certainty something was amiss with Belenus had roused him from his bed. Not that he'd slept, tormented by the dilemmas he faced.

He should raise the alarm, but Brig's rescue of Cadha might solve one of his problems. From the direction the pair had gone, he'd guess the plan was to take his betrothed back to the Abbey. Why hadn't he thought of that? While he'd been mired in worry, the courageous Brigandine had acted. She had risked everything for her childhood friend, though she'd intimated they had never been close, their social class being too disparate.

Something had pushed her to ride off with Cadha. Mayhap she understood his desperate wish to protect the innocent postulant from an agonizing death. Or was there another reason?

He considered his own motives. Did he abhor the notion of wedding Cadha simply because of the curse? Or was there someone else he wanted for wife? Someone he burned for, someone with tufts of red hair.

He cursed himself for a fool. All he had to do was wed a sweet, stammering girl with a lazy eye, fight off her vengeful father, aid in the building of a castle, impress King William and thus King Henry, and live happily ever after. But his heart recognised that true happiness lay with Brigandine Lordsmith.

"Go with God," he rasped before returning to his bed, confident Belenus would be contentedly munching oats in his stall by daybreak.

# FIRE

Brig ambled along the pathway back to the castle atop Belenus. A radiant Sister Cadha had given basic instructions on how to control the animal, but she'd soon realized she didn't need them. The horse knew where it was supposed to go.

She thought back to their arrival at the Abbey. It came as a relief when the Bishop greeted them, ranting and raving about the heathen English and their barbaric Scots cronies.

He was only too willing to proceed with Cadha's ordination into the sisterhood. She remembered the ceremony she'd been privileged to witness in the chapel. She was part of something wondrous as Gilbride's daughter swore her vows to Christ.

*I would dedicate my life to Matthew. If only it were possible.*

She gazed at the pinks and reds of the sunrise, filled with a fanciful notion she was heading for an enchanted land where she and Matthew—

It came to her suddenly that she was traveling west; the sun was rising behind her, but the sky ahead was ablaze. Belenus pricked up his ears. "Something's burning," she whispered to the beast.

The horse took off like a bolt from a crossbow. She clung to his mane, fearing for life and limb if she tumbled to the ground. Despite her fear, it came to her that animals ran away from fires. Belenus sensed danger —to his master.

She urged him on then. "Faster, faster."

~ ~ ~

After watching Cadha's escape, Matthew returned to his chamber, not even bothering to disrobe. He fell into a fitful doze, dreaming of Brig's magnificent breasts. He conjured a vision of her with long hair, down to her waist. The hair at her mons was likely the same fiery red. He'd find out when—

An insistent banging at the door jolted him upright. He raked his fingers through his hair. Someone was calling his name. "*Commandante* de Rowenne. *Fuego*!"

Fire?

He smelled it then. Burning wood. Was the castle ablaze? He thrust open the door, buckling on his sword. "Are we under attack?" he asked the Aragonese.

"*Sì, sì, foresta, fuego*," the soldier replied as they hastened along the hallway.

Gilbride had evidently torched the dense forest surrounding Lincluden as a distraction before his assault. It wouldn't take long before the flames licked at the castle itself.

His thoughts went to the stables and he thanked the saints Belenus was safe.

He rushed out to the rear of the castle where the forge stood. Gorrie and Brig lived above it. He had to be sure she hadn't returned. He caught sight of the armorer down near the river. It appeared he had organised a line of men that stretched from the water to the castle. They passed pails one to the other. Matthew hurried to his side. "Brig?" he asked hoarsely.

"Nowhere to be found," her father grunted.

It occurred to Matthew that here was Gilbride's armorer trying to prevent the flames reaching the castle. "Good man, Gorrie," he said, slapping the burly giant on the shoulder.

The smith eyed him. "Aye, well, it came to me I dinna hold wi' a man murderin' his ain brother. What's to keep 'im from killin' anyone he tecks a fancy to killin'?"

Matthew might have retorted that even King Henry might do away with anyone he *took a fancy* to killing, but he held his peace.

"Besides," Gorrie went on, "this be my home now, mine and Brig's, and ye English hae bin decent wi' us, even that Cordier. But ye best tell him to keep his eyes off my lad."

He strode away, leaving Matthew dumfounded. Had Le Cordier discovered Brig's secret, or was he—

No time to think on that. Gilbride's army might emerge any minute now the flames in the trees had died down. The heavy smoke would provide good cover.

Coughing, he made his way around the outer perimeter of the castle, making sure sparks hadn't caught. Eyes watering, he ran into the bailey. The stables at the far end were engulfed in flame. Some horses that had apparently been saved were down near the Nith. A few animals pranced nervously around the bailey, whinnying and snorting.

If the attack came now, they'd have no chance. Where was Le Cordier? Why hadn't a defence been organised?

The answer came when his *Capitaine* stumbled out of the keep, tucking his shirt into his leggings. Surely the arrogant nobleman hadn't slept through the racket?

He decided there was no time to waste on recriminations. "Where is King William?" he shouted.

Le Cordier bent over, hacking up phlegm. Once he caught his breath he panted, "I advised him to stay in his chamber. Safer there."

Matthew nodded, but he'd never been in a dangerous situation that was so out of control, and he didn't like it. "We should have been prepared for this," he growled at his *Capitaine*. "We underestimated Gilbride."

Still coughing, Le Cordier agreed. "I didn't think he had enough men to launch an assault."

Matthew's eyes darted here and there, scanning the smoking forest for any sign of attack, pleased to see the *routiers* regrouping, taking up a defensive position. Perhaps there wasn't going to be an assault after all. But why set fire to—?

*Not enough men.*

"Their plan wasn't to attack the castle," he shouted to Le Cordier as he ran to the Keep. "They are already inside. Send a party of Aragonese to follow me to the King's chamber."

"But William is well guarded," Le Cordier shouted after him.

Heart pounding, sword in hand, Matthew took the stone steps to the second floor two at a time. As he feared, three of William's guards lay slumped against the frame of the door to the royal chamber. It was small consolation that two of the enemy also lay dead. Afraid he'd arrived too late he entered the chamber cautiously.

The king was fending off a youth. William wielded a sword. His attacker, armed with a dagger, had backed his quarry into a corner.

A glint in the king's eye indicated he'd seen Matthew enter.

*Probably the first time we've been glad to see each other.*

Matthew lay his sword on the bed, and crept up behind the lad, clamping one arm around his neck. As the boy staggered backwards, Matthew grabbed his wrist and twisted hard, forcing the dagger to fall. The youth yelped in pain.

William pressed the point of his sword to his chest. "Yield," he shouted.

Matthew privately thought the regal bravado somewhat late since he'd already subdued and disarmed the assailant, but let the king believe he'd vanquished his would-be assassin. He thrust the scowling lad into the hands of one of the Aragonese who burst into the chamber. It came to him where he'd seen him before. "Make sure he doesn't escape this time. We need information."

The youth spat at him. "I'll never tell ye aught."

Matthew had a strange feeling this was one of the youths who'd attacked Brig. He burned to slap him hard across the face. Men who raped women were cowards. They didn't last long under torture. "Take him away," he said.

As the color returned to his ashen face, the king sheathed his sword. "My thanks, Matthew de Rowenne. I owe you my life. Now let's see what's happening with the defences."

He disappeared out the door, leaving Matthew

standing dumbfounded. He shook his head. Every time he came into contact with King William the Lion, something unexpected happened. Mayhap the saints were looking out for him after all. He now had a second king in his debt, though the rewards from the first had been dubious at best.

He reached to retrieve his sword, and felt cold steel pressed to his neck.

# SAINT GEORGE

"Hands in the air," a gravelly voice hissed.

The blade pressed further into Matthew's flesh. One wrong move and he'd be dead, his throat cut. "The fight is lost," he said as he complied, trying not to let his fear show. "There's no escape. If—"

Something, he suspected a meaty fist, struck him hard on the back of the neck. The blow sent him reeling. His assailant kicked him hard, over and over. He curled into a ball to protect himself.

When the kicking finally stopped, he waited, wondering if any of the Aragonese lingered nearby. His attacker had the dagger, and Matthew's sword. Struggling not to surrender to the oblivion that would ease the agony, he half expected to feel the bite of the blade he should have kept to hand. He spat out the bitter taste of his own blood.

A foot poked him. "Get up."

He got to his knees. The pain was intense. It felt like every bone in his body was broken. Breathing was nigh on impossible.

"Get. Up."

He was grabbed by the arm and hoisted to his feet. Eye to eye with his attacker for the first time, he thought of trying to wrestle with the youth. But the brute was big and strong, and in his condition he'd stand no chance. Where were the Aragonese?

The knife was placed against his neck again and his arm twisted behind his back.

"We'll walk out o' here, slowly. Ye'll be my shield."

He hadn't the strength to tell the fool the *routiers* would cut him down. Sacrificing Matthew's life would mean nothing to them.

It pained him that he hadn't told Brigandine of his love for her before he died. The irony of it. He'd been preoccupied with the haunting memory of his mother's death and failed to grasp the promise that life with the courageous Brig offered.

He later had no memory of making it down the steps, nor of crossing the Hall, nor of stepping through the outer door of the Keep into the bailey. But as long as he lived he would never forget his wonderment when Saint George of the Golden Legend appeared, riding a red dragon, resplendent in his suit of shining armor. The snorting beast fixed a steely eye on him and he knew all would be well.

~~~

"Unhand him, Hamish," Brig growled as she slid from the snorting Belenus, sword in hand.

Strangely, she wasn't afraid of the bully who'd brutalized her, but she feared for Matthew. He'd been badly beaten and looked about ready to drop.

Hamish's eyes darted here and there. It was evident he was struggling to keep his prisoner upright.

"Unhand him," she said again. "And surrender to me."

Hamish snorted. "Nay, Brig Lordsmith, I'll nay

surrender to the likes o' ye. Dinna come closer or I'll kill him."

She took a step forward, unbuckling the overly large belt of the scabbard, and tossing it aside. She'd look the fool if it fell to her ankles and she tripped over it. "Nay, Hamish. If ye kill him, where is yer shield? These men ye see gathering behind me, they'll cut ye doon like a wee sapling and hack ye to pieces."

His eyes roved over the Aragonese she sensed had assembled around her. She could smell as well as hear them. "They'll kill me anyway," he rasped.

"Nay, Hamish. If ye unhand him, 'twill be me and thee, a sword fight to the death. If ye win I guarantee yer freedom. William, King o' all Scotland is here, and he'll see they bide by what I say."

She hoped the king was in fact behind her and that he understood Gaelic. Relief surged up her spine when a regal voice declared, "I so bear witness."

Matthew babbled something about Saint George, wincing when Hamish forced his arm further up his back. Brig feared he'd soon succumb to his injuries.

"Let him go," she repeated, pleased to see an arrogant glint appear in Hamish's eye. He might be good with his fists, but he was no swordsman.

"I'll kill ye quick," he crowed. "After all ye're just a lass and ye look like a toy soldier in that costume."

That did it.

"Let him go," she hissed, "and we'll see who is the lass."

There was laughter from the Aragonese, though she doubted they understood what had been said. Evidently they respected her bravado.

Hamish unexpectedly shoved Matthew aside and lunged for her. She'd no time to see if he'd slashed her beloved's throat. The fight was on for her own life now she'd hopefully saved Matthew's.

The point of his sword stung her arm, sharpening her determination to win. She thrust and parried and feinted and ducked, remembering everything her father had ever taught her. She twirled, whirled and danced, her feet taking on a life of their own. She poked Hamish on the arse. He squealed, his sweating face red with indignation. The bystanders howled.

She thanked the saints for the strength in her arms and legs, strength born of a lifetime of hard work. Her opponent tired quickly as she evaded his every attempt to land a blow. When he could barely lift his sword, she flicked it out of his grip and lunged hard for his shoulder. He howled in pain, crashing to the ground as blood spurted from the deep wound she inflicted.

"That'll teach ye to mess with girls," she taunted amid cheers from the onlookers.

Hamish was hauled away. She didn't have it in her to finish him off, but doubted he'd leave Lincluden alive. She picked up the dagger he'd dropped. Her dagger.

Suddenly she was in her gleeful father's beefy arms. "I'm proud o' ye, Brig. Ye were payin' attention after all."

All her life she'd longed to hear words of praise from her father. She hugged him, but her concern was for Matthew.

"They've taken him to the healer," her Da explained. "Broken ribs, I'd say."

She handed him her weapons and hurried off to tend

the man she loved.

# THE MOTH

The castle's healer ushered Brigandine into Matthew's chamber. He lay on his bed, as still as death. His garments had been removed. A linen sheet covered the lower part of his body. She suspected he was naked beneath it.

His cheekbones were bruised. An angry red line betrayed where the dagger had dug into his neck. But his body—

Brig licked salty tears that ran unbidden down her face. Every inch of his broad chest was mottled red with bruises. She fervently hoped he'd not been kicked below the belt.

"Dinna cry, laddie," the healer chided. "He's a braw man. He'll recover, God willin'."

"I'm nay a laddie," she murmured in response, "and I'll cry for the man I love if I wish."

Leighis eyed her curiously. "Ha! Always suspicioned there was summat funny about ye, Brig Lordsmith. When ye first came from Cruggleton, I said to—-" She wiped Matthew's forehead with a wet cloth then narrowed her eyes at Brig—"Weel, doesna matter now what I said. Would ye like to bathe his face?"

Brig accepted the linen with trembling hands and nervously dabbed Matthew's forehead. "My love," she whispered.

He blinked open bleary eyes. "Brigandine?" he rasped.

"Aye, I'm here."

He took her hand and pressed it to his lips. "Thank God," he whispered. "I dreamt you were in a sword fight. Saint George saved you. He came on his red dragon."

"Ye didna dream it," Leighis interjected, winking at Brig. "He fought Hamish the Bully-boy and won handily. Did ye know Brig's a lass?" She guffawed loudly, slapping her thigh. "O' course ye did!"

Matthew smiled weakly then closed his eyes and swallowed hard. Brig watched him fight the pain, wishing she could take it from him.

The healer gently lifted his head and held an unstoppered *potel* to his lips. "A few swigs o' *dwale* and ye'll feel no pain," she said. "Just a bit, mind."

Matthew grimaced as he swallowed the bitter potion, and Brig was instantly worried. She'd heard of folk adding too much hemlock or henbane to their dwale recipe. "'Tis yer ain concoction, I trust," she asked Leighis. "Ye ken what's in it?"

The woman bristled. "Listen, laddie, or lassie, or whate'er ye be. I've been the healer in this castle since before ye were born and I've ne'er poisoned anybody yet. Now shoo while I bind this man's broken bones."

Brig gripped the side of the mattress. "Nay. I'll stay to help ye."

~~~

Matthew made a valiant effort to keep his eyes open. As long as the beautiful face framed by red tufts was before him, all would be well. But the dwale quickly carried him out of his pain. Drifting into oblivion, he wondered if he'd told her he loved her. He'd meant to. It had been the last thing on his mind before Saint George had appeared.

She and the healer were binding his chest. He liked the notion of her small hands on him. If she ran them all over his body he'd die a happy man. He chuckled. Ironic. He and Brig, both with bindings around their chests. Of course, his was because he'd broken a rib or two. Her bindings concealed breasts. He planned to unwind hers and suckle at the first opportunity. He licked his lips. Dwale made a man thirsty—and hot.

~ ~ ~

"He's raving," Brig whispered. "Are ye sure about the dwale? He thinks we're taking the bindings off."

Leighis remained stern faced, her concentration on her work. "Dinna fash. He'll mend. We hafta guard agin' fever, and pray there's naught else damaged inside. Keep his brow cool."

Brig dipped the linen in the water bowl, wrung it out and wiped the sweat beading on Matthew's forehead. To her relief he smiled. Did he know she was there, or had the potion carried him off to a land of dreams?

"Brigandine," he rasped, licking his lips.

She'd never kissed or been kissed before, but his mouth drew her. When Leighis turned away to replenish the water from the ewer, she leaned over and brushed her lips over his, smoothing a lock of hair off his face. She tasted the bitter dwale, but he parted his lips slightly and his breath mingled with hers. The softness, the sweetness, the wicked exhilaration of joining her mouth to his filled her with joy.

He growled in his sleep and unexpectedly sucked her tongue into his mouth. Some alchemy flooded her body with joy, with need, with wanting.

A desire to moan with happiness rose in her throat.

"Careful, or ye'll press too hard on his chest."

She jolted backwards, fearing the healer's censure for her actions.

Matthew whimpered like a child deprived of something it craves.

"The love o' a good woman oft helps a wounded man heal," Leighis said. "Dinna be afraid to put yer hands on him."

She bustled out of the chamber.

Brig stared at Matthew. She longed to touch him. What better time than when he was asleep. He'd never know. Holding her breath, she put her hands on his shoulders then traced the contours of his arms with her fingertips, exploring the muscles, savoring the soft hair on his forearms. Letting out a ragged breath, she lifted a hand and interlaced her fingers with his, awed by the size and texture of his palm. His hands were powerful, yet gentle. She rested his fingers on her lips, then sucked one into her mouth, tasting salt and desire.

He stirred in his sleep, sending a flutter scurrying up her spine. She carefully put his hand down by his side and stared at the shape of his legs beneath the sheet. Her fingers twitched. She chewed her bottom lip. Mayhap if she lifted the sheet and just looked at his feet. He'd seen her feet, so why not?

She stood at the foot of the bed and picked up the edge of the linen raising it just enough to reveal his knees. She remembered sitting in his lap in the druid circle, and pressing her thighs to his atop Belenus. She could peek at those wondrous thighs. No harm in that. She raised the linen. Her eyes travelled along the line of muscle, until they fell on a nest of black curls. His male parts lay at rest. A vision of him standing naked in the Nith played behind her eyes. He hadn't lain at rest then, despite the cold water!

"He's a bonnie man."

She dropped the linen, fire racing through her veins. She'd been engrossed in her exploration and hadn't heard Leighis return to the chamber.

The healer chuckled. "Naught to be ashamed of. He's the kind of man who attracts women like moths to the flame."

The truth of it struck Brig like a lightning bolt. She was the moth drawn to Matthew's flame, and it was the fire of love that consumed her. If she became his wife, she wasn't going to die a fiery death. She already had, but her true self had emerged from the ashes. Now to convince him of it.

# CHOICES

For the next fortnight, Brig spent every free moment tending Matthew. Leighis had pronounced he was on the mend and allowed him to get up and walk for a few minutes.

She relished his weight as he leaned on her for support. "You're strong—for a girl," he teased.

She kept him abreast of events. "All of Lincluden is agog with gossip about your heroic rescue of the King of Scotland, the sword fight, and the revelation I'm a female."

She'd told him of the duel with Hamish. He couldn't seem to get enough of the tale and had her repeat it over and over, asking more than once if she was sure Saint George hadn't been there.

"The problem of my leaving the forge has been solved," she told him. "Dozens of lads have swamped Gorrie, begging to be taken on as his apprentice. He's chosen one. He beams with pride whene'er he sets eyes on me, though I've a feeling something is on his mind. I dinna see much of him, what with the new boy."

He paused in his walking and ogled her. "No wonder he looks at you with pride now you're dressed as a woman, and your hair is growing. I can't wait to see it down to your waist."

She felt the blush rise in her cheeks under his admiring gaze. "Aye. I expected censure from the lasses of the castle, but instead I'm the object of admiration and the recipient of several comely *lèines*, chemises and shoes. It seemed strange at first, but I dinna miss the uncomfortable bindings around my chest."

He sat heavily on the edge of the mattress. "I'll be glad to get mine off too. I suppose men are drifting back to Lincluden after the news Gilbride has sued for peace with William the Lion."

"Aye," she agreed, helping him back into bed, "I'm saddened my homeland is to become part of the kingdom of Scotland, but William has proven himself a better leader than Gilbride."

Matthew took her hand. "Your land will prosper under the protection of William and King Henry. Leighis told me Gilbride will be named Earl of Galloway and allowed to keep Cruggleton Castle in return for swearing homage to William."

"Where does the woman get this news?" she asked. "She's always first to know."

He smiled. "Mayhap she has the king's ear."

They laughed together. It elated her to see him on the mend. "The general opinion is that once the castle at Dumfries is completed, Lincluden will be abandoned."

He shrugged, then winced. "Wish I hadn't done that," he quipped. "Dumfries. Who knows how long before I can assist with that grand project? William will probably send me back to Henry."

"That would break my heart," she murmured.

He squeezed her hand. "I love you, Brigandine, and I'm beginning to see the wisdom of your explanation of

ANNA MARKLAND

the legacy of the red glass, but even if you're right, things are uncertain—"

She snatched her hand from his grip. "Ye're the man for me, Matthew de Rowenne. There'll be no other. If I canna be yer wife, that will be the hell I'll burn in. But I'm beginning to get the feeling yer reluctance has more to do with the fact I'm the daughter of a—"

A loud rap at the door drew their attention. He leaned back on the bolster, his eyes full of sadness that tore at her heart. "*Entrez*," he rasped.

A Spanish mercenary entered and bowed. "*El Rey* William has summoned—"

Matthew held up a hand. "Tell His Majesty it will take me a few minutes to get there. I'll need your help."

The soldier shook his head. "No, *Commandante* de Rowenne. It is the lady he wishes to see."

~~~

Matthew lay back and worried.

Why had the King of Scotland summoned Brigandine? It could only be to give her a reward of some kind. Surely she wasn't to be punished for masquerading as a man. If anyone deserved punishment for the ruse it was Gorrie Lordsmith.

She'd turned fearful eyes on him when she'd left, as if she might never see him again.

The prospect gnawed at his vitals. Brigandine had become essential to his happiness. She claimed to be the moth drawn to his flame, yet he couldn't foresee a life without her.

She was strong, courageous. She'd saved his life. He'd been attracted to her even before he'd known she was a woman, his body wiser than his brain. If ever there was a moth consumed by the flames of love, it was him.

But he'd striven for so long to distance himself from humble ancestors, to climb the social ladder. Mayhap she was right. He was too proud to wed with her. King Henry would be disinclined to bestow rewards on a man married to a tradesman's daughter.

The choice was clear. Ambition or love.

~~~

Brigandine teetered nervously upon entering the king's antechamber, not only because William the Lion sat before her, but Gorrie Lordsmith knelt at his feet. She had never curtseyed and hoped she wouldn't fall over.

"Rise," the king said. "I see your hair is growing."

This she hadn't expected.

He pointed to his own hair. "Same color as mine."

She'd never paid much attention to his appearance before, except to note he was a big man. She often wondered at the strength it must have taken for Matthew to unhorse and subdue him. "Aye," she murmured, then hastily added, "Yer Majesty."

He chuckled. "Strange, isn't it, that your father doesn't have red hair?"

She looked at Gorrie's rigid back. Something was wrong.

The king retrieved a small rolled parchment from inside his gambeson. "Your father has presented me with this document."

This didn't make sense. Gorrie could neither read nor write.

William must have perceived her confusion. "You are right in thinking he had no notion what was written upon it."

He turned his gaze on Gorrie. "Tell me, master armorer, did your wife have red hair?"

*Aye! Down to her waist. He's often told me—*

"Nay, Yer Majesty," her father rasped.

Brig had heard tell of tentacled creatures that swam in the sea. One splashed about in her innards.

The king spoke again. "Your father has kept this document for seventeen, mayhap eighteen years. How old are you?"

The creature was swimming its way up her throat. "I'll turn eighteen at harvest time."

"He found it in a basket left at his forge."

An urge to run for the door seized her. She didn't want to hear the King's next words.

"There was a child in the basket, a babe."

*Nay! Nay! Nay!*

"Gorrie Lordsmith and his wife were childless. They saw the babe as a gift from God. As the lass grew they believed there was less chance of her being reclaimed if they pretended she was a boy."

Gorrie was sobbing. She could bear it no longer. "Nay!" she screamed. "He's my Da. He loves me."

"Of course he loves you. That's why he kept the secret all these years. But he's a truthful man and thus the reason for the letter's continued existence. Am I right, Armorer?"

"Aye," Gorrie whispered.

William the Lion unfurled the parchment and cleared his throat, preparing to read the words that she feared would change her life forever.

*Nurture this child of my heart, a bastard born of my love for a soldier. If my lord betrothed discovers the truth he will slay us all. Tell her of my love.*

The chamber tilted. The creature was tearing her heart to shreds. She swayed, grateful as she surrendered to oblivion that Gorrie Lordsmith's strong arms prevented her from crashing to the tiled floor.

# THE TEST

Gorrie carried Brig to the cramped rooms they inhabited over the forge. Once she'd recovered her wits, she contemplated her new circumstances. All she'd heard of the letter initially was that she was a bastard, a child born out of wedlock, an outcast.

But it seemed her real mother had been of the nobility, a woman who'd fallen in love with a soldier and given herself to him though betrothed to another. A soldier! How ironic! The man mayhap didn't even know he had a daughter.

Her mother had loved her.

Gorrie blubbered, on his knees beside her pallet, begging forgiveness.

She sat up, cupped his face in her hands and kissed his forehead. "There is naught to forgive, Da. I ne'er had any inkling ye weren't my real father. I know ye love me."

He put his big hands over her wrists. "Mayhap now de Rowenne will take ye to wife."

Her heart careened around her ribcage. She didn't want Matthew to wed her because she might have a smidgen of noble blood in her veins. She loved him unconditionally and that wouldn't change even if he were a blacksmith.

She scrambled to her feet when they heard footsteps on the ladder leading to their garret. Gorrie grovelled when King William's red head appeared, a broad grin on his face.

"Get up, man," he commanded, suddenly filling the tiny hovel.

Gorrie struggled to his feet. "Yer Majesty, this is no place for a king."

William waved him off. "I was anxious to see if Brigandine had recovered from her shock."

She nodded. "I have, Yer Majesty."

"Good," he replied. "You left before I had a chance to convey the second part of my news."

She furrowed her brow. The first news had been momentous enough.

"You may have heard that I intend my new castle at Dumfries to become the main fortification in these parts," the king began. "Lincluden will be more or less abandoned."

She risked a nod of understanding, unsure where this was leading.

"However, I don't want Gilbride to get his hands on Lincluden. The place will require a Master, or mayhap a Chatelaine."

Gorrie gaped.

Brig remained silent.

"Matthew de Rowenne would make a fine Master, but I have other duties in mind for him."

Brigandine grew uncomfortable beneath the king's sudden steely-eyed glare. Was he expecting some kind of reaction on her part to the news Matthew was to be rewarded. "He's a fine man," she murmured.

"Ha!" William retorted. "Is that all you've got to say about the man you risked your life to save? Here I am on the verge of investing you as Lady of Lincluden so that he can marry you—"

She supposed it was the tears rolling down her face that silenced the monarch.

"Why are you crying? It's a great honor I'm bestowing on you."

She swallowed, hoping she didn't sound ungrateful. "I am deeply honored," she explained, "but I dinna want Matthew to wed with me simply because ye've given me a title."

The king stroked his beard. "I see. True love and all that."

"Aye," she murmured.

Gorrie scurried out of William's way as he made for the ladder, but the king turned to her before descending. "Brigandine Lordsmith, I hereby invest you with the title Lady of Lincluden, and I pray you attend me in the Great Hall forthwith."

He was gone before she could protest.

Her heart was in knots. She would never succeed as a Lady without Matthew as her helpmate.

~~~

Matthew's injuries were healing well. He felt stronger by the minute. But he hadn't seen Brigandine for days and every moment spent apart from her was an eternity.

Leighis was tight-lipped about what had transpired when Brig had been summoned before the king, though he suspected she knew. All she would say was, "Ye'll find out soon enough." He wasn't sure if the strange look in her eye meant he'd be pleased when he found out or—

He resolved to seek an audience with the king. He'd saved the man's life after all. William had admitted he owed Matthew a debt. As his reward he'd beg forgiveness for whatever Brig was being punished for. He'd ask for her hand in marriage. It would likely mean bidding adieu to his dreams of advancement, and a knighthood would be out of the question, but Brigandine was right. He was the man for her.

He sent word through Leighis he wished to speak with the king. An answer came more quickly than he anticipated. "Help me dress," he growled to the woman whose skills had helped him heal.

She glowered in reply, arms folded across her copious bosom.

"I apologise," he breathed. "I am anxious, and I cannot go to the king robed in a nightshirt."

The healer fetched his garments. He got his leggings and boots on with some difficulty.

"Take off the bindings," he said, feeling as weak as a babe.

"Nay," she replied adamantly. "Not time."

It was futile to argue. He'd tried it before.

Dressing exhausted him. "I doubt I can walk to the Hall," he admitted. "Call one of the *routiers* to assist me."

"Nay," she replied. "Ye can lean on me."

A man reliant on the support of an old woman was sure to impress the king. But what choice did he have?

They made their slow way to the Hall. He bowed as best he could before William who was seated in the Lord's Chair. To his relief a servant brought a stool and placed it a few feet in front of the King's. "Sit," the monarch commanded, waving Leighis away.

She pouted but obeyed and left the Hall.

A peat fire smoked in the grate. Matthew had never seen peat burning until he'd first come to Scotland. He filled his lungs with the comforting, earthy aroma.

William stared at him, his fingers steepled under his bearded chin. Matthew got the strange feeling they weren't alone, but supposed there were likely guards lurking in the shadows.

"You asked for an audience," the king said flatly.

His tone worried Matthew. Had the man forgotten his promise of a reward?

"I did, Your Majesty," he replied.

"Come to seek your reward."

It wasn't a question. A nervous shiver crept across Matthew's nape. For some inexplicable reason he felt he'd been kicked in the ribs, again. Nevertheless, he had a purpose in coming and he intended to fulfill it. "I ask only one thing," he replied.

"What is that? Command of Dumfries perhaps? It's yours for the taking."

Matthew was thunderstruck.

"Or mayhap a knighthood?" the king added. "Which goes without saying since only a knight can command a castle such as Dumfries."

It was everything he'd ever wanted, thirsted for, dreamed of. But in reality that was no longer true. He cleared his throat. "Before you bestow such honors on me, Your Majesty, do not think me ungrateful, but you need to know I have come to ask permission to marry."

William narrowed his eyes. "A knight can marry."

Matthew inhaled deeply, causing his ribs to spasm. "The woman I wish to wed is the armorer's daughter, Brigandine Lordsmith."

He wasn't sure what to expect, but a hearty grin wasn't among the possibilities. Did the king think his injuries had addled his wits?

"Why don't you ask her yourself?" William suggested, looking off to the shadows.

His heart leaped into his throat when Brig emerged from an alcove. He got up from the chair, sore ribs forgotten, and walked to her side. He took her hands in his. "Will you wed with me, Brigandine? Will you let the fire of my love consume you?"

"Gladly," she murmured in reply, a naughty glint in her eye. "Since ye asked me before ye knew."

"Knew what?" he rasped, wondering if it was appropriate to run his hands over her body in the presence of a king.

"That's she's of noble blood," William shouted, leaping from his chair.

Matthew staggered under the blow the king clamped on his shoulder. Retaliation he supposed for the chains on the journey to Normandie. "I don't understand," he said.

"A wonderful portent for peace," William declared.

Matthew was just as befuddled. "Portent?"

"The marriage of the Anglo-Norman Commander of Dumfries, Sir Matthew de Rowenne and Lady Brigandine Lordsmith, Chatelaine of Lincluden, Galloway born and bred."

Brig smiled and linked her arm with his. "Yer face is as red as a winter beetroot. Ye look like yer on fire."

Matthew didn't understand how it could be that Brig had become a Lady, and he didn't care. He gazed into the eyes of the woman he loved but thought he'd never have. "I am," he replied.

# A WEDDING

Despite his animosity towards King William, Bishop Mortimer agreed to offer the nuptial mass at Lincluden Abbey "for Brigandine Lordsmith's sake."

"I hope the king thinks the Bishop's respect for you is because you now have oversight of the Abbey, and not because you helped Cadha escape," Matthew whispered as they came together at the door of the chapel to exchange vows.

Her eyes widened. "You knew?"

He chuckled. "I sensed something was amiss with Belenus. I saw you ride off."

"Good thing Cadha knew how to control a horse," she replied with a laugh that turned into a snort.

The Bishop eyed her with disapproval.

"She's simply nervous," Matthew explained, which seemed to appease the old cleric.

Brig screwed up her nose at him in disapproval. "I am not nervous," she hissed.

Matthew rolled his eyes. "Very ladylike," he quipped. "Remember there's a king present."

She straightened her shoulders and pursed her lips, obviously trying not to laugh as the Bishop began the rite that would bind him to the fascinating creature he loved.

He too wanted to shout out his joy. The wit and common sense and love of an urchin who'd spent her life working in a forge had helped him see that his legacy wasn't tainted by any curse. It was simply a remarkable piece of jewellery that she'd insisted he wear today. Her biggest worry seemed to be what they'd do if she bore only girls and no sons. "We'll dress one of them up as a boy and give it to her," had been his reply.

Thinking back on the giggling and tickling that had gone on after that remark had him pleasantly aroused. He'd enjoyed it despite some tenderness that remained in his ribs.

*How much longer before I can strip off the green satin gown?*

He suddenly realized the bishop was looking at him expectantly. He wasn't sure what question he'd been asked. "I so swear," he said with great solemnity in the hope that was the right answer.

Apparently it was!

Brigandine swore her vows in such a sultry voice, he wondered how he could ever have thought she was a boy.

They processed into the chapel for the mass, then walked amid a crowd of cheering well-wishers back to the castle.

~~~

Brigandine had never imbibed wine, and would have preferred to keep a clear head for what lay ahead after the wedding banquet, but when an inebriated king offers a goblet or two of the *finest brought from his cellars in Scone*—what's a woman to do?

She felt the effects of the heady wine as Matthew

carried her to his chamber. He'd insisted, despite his newly healed injuries. "I'm going to carry my bride over the threshold if it kills me," he stated flatly.

He rubbed his ribs once he'd deposited her on her feet next to the big bed, leading her to believe it had been a strain for him. She made a mock curtsey. "Thank you, kind sir."

He returned the gesture with a courtly bow. "Anything for my Lady," he jested.

Another first for her was the notion of sleeping in a proper bed. He chuckled as she walked around the four poster, trailing her hand over the bedspread. "It's beautiful," she murmured.

He cupped her face in his hands and pressed his manhood to her mons. "You are the thing of beauty in this chamber, Brig. Thank you for being my wife. Are you nervous?"

He had sensed her uncertainty. "I am, though the wine relaxed me a little, but I havna had much practice being a woman."

His arousal hardened at her words. "I will be happy to teach you," he rasped. "Do you know what will happen this night?"

Emboldened by the wine, she reached down and stroked the back of her fingers against his manhood. "Leighis said it has something to do with this."

He put his arms around her, trapping her hand against him, his hips thrusting gently. "She was right," he murmured, nuzzling her ear.

She stepped away from his embrace and touched fingertips to her mons. "And this," she whispered, wishing she had the courage to tell him of the need that throbbed there, of the wet heat.

He inhaled, his eyes darkening. "Again the healer was right, and I'll wager you are already wet for me."

*He knew!*

He cupped her breasts, brushing his thumbs over the nipples. Her longing intensified.

"I have thirsted to look upon you again after the night in the druid circle," he said. "You cannot know how relieved I was to discover you're a woman."

"Relieved?"

"Lusting for a boy is worrisome for a warrior," he quipped with a rueful smile.

"Ye lusted for me, even before?"

"Almost from the first moment I met you," he admitted.

She put her hands on her hips, elated by his admission. "This bears out what I've kept telling ye. We are destined to be together. I fought my attraction to ye thinking I didna need a man."

He pressed his forehead to hers. "And do you need one now?"

"What I feel is more than need, Matthew. I burn with love for ye."

He growled, his lips on her neck. Once more the wine brought out a naughtiness she didn't know she possessed. "And I long to see that magnificent male part o' yers—again."

His eyes widened. "That's right. I forgot you saw me naked at the river."

Did she dare tell him?

"Aye, and again after that," she teased.

He teased her nipples, a curious smile tugging at the

114

corners of his mouth. "Tell me."

A spark of guilty pleasure fanned the flames of desire. "When ye were lying witless after the beating. I lifted the linen and peeked."

His eyes danced. "You took advantage of an injured man?"

"Aye," she laughed. "I enjoyed it."

"I suppose I'll have to show it to you again," he quipped, untying the laces of his leggings and shoving them down over his hips. She was completely unprepared for what sprang forth, but an inner voice pushed her to curl her hand around him. "Leighis was right again. Ye are a bonnie man," she said hoarsely.

She must have looked nervous.

"Don't worry," he said. "It will fit. I'll prepare you."

She had no notion what he meant, but was anxious for preparations to begin.

~~~

Matthew had Brig sit on the edge of the mattress while he quickly shucked his boots and tore off his leggings. From the way she was swaying he feared she might topple over if she didn't sit down. The doublet and shirt came off in a trice, but before tossing the doublet to the floor, he slowly unpinned the brooch. He stood before her, the jewel in his palm.

"Ye're naked," she whispered, raking her eyes over his body.

"And the idea is we both be naked," he jested, handing her the pin. "Hold on to it—for courage."

She came to her feet and he undressed her slowly, tossing her garments and shoes to the four corners of the chamber. He had a feeling she was concerned about his treatment of her new finery and the mess, but she held her tongue. It was going to be interesting living with a woman who wasn't used to having servants.

He brought their bodies together, relishing her soft curves, her warmth. He slid his shaft between her thighs. "You're hot and wet," he rasped.

She responded to his slow rhythm, clinging to him. "This feels wonderful," she said. "It does fit."

She must have felt his erection buck at the innocence of her words. He certainly did.

"This is only the beginning," he replied, lifting her on to the bed. "Open your legs for me."

She averted her shy gaze as he stared at her most intimate place. He should explain to her what he was about to do but might babble like a lunatic. The promise of her soft pink folds had his heart beating too fast. "Trust me," was all he could manage.

She startled when he put his lips on her, but he anchored his arms around her thighs and suckled and licked, revelling in her sweet female taste. Soon she moaned and whimpered, tossing her head from side to side on the bolster.

When she screamed out her fulfillment, he came to his knees, closed his eyes and gently slid inside her throbbing sheath. She was tight, despite the wet heat, and he went slowly, deeper and deeper until he felt her maidenhead tear.

Close to completion, he opened his eyes. She was staring at him, a smile of utter joy on her face, his legacy nestled between her breasts.

Love consumed him as his seed erupted inside her.

# PASSION'S FIRE

# ABOUT ANNA

Thank you for reading *PASSION'S FIRE*. If you'd like to leave a review where you purchased the book, and/or on Goodreads, I would appreciate it. Reviews contribute greatly to an author's success.

I'd love you to visit my <u>website</u> and my Facebook page, <u>Anna Markland Novels</u>.

Tweet me @annamarkland, join me on <u>Pinterest</u>, or sign up for my <u>newsletter</u>.

Passion smolders in my page-turning adventures, turning to ashes whatever obstacles a hostile medieval world can throw in its path.

Besides writing, I have two addictions-crosswords and genealogy, probably the reason I love research. I am a fool for cats. My husband is an entrepreneur who is fond of boasting he's never had a job.

I live on Canada's scenic west coast now, but I was born and raised in the UK and I love breathing life into the history of my homeland.

Escape with me to where romance began.

# MORE MARKLAND

If you prefer to read sagas in chronological order, here's a handy list for the Montbryce family books.

Conquering Passion—Ram and Mabelle, Rhodri and Rhonwen

If Love Dares Enough—Hugh and Devona, Antoine and Sybilla

Defiant Passion-Rhodri and Rhonwen

A Man of Value—Caedmon and Agneta

Dark Irish Knight—Ronan and Rhoni

Haunted Knights—Adam and Rosamunda, Denis and Paulina

Passion in the Blood—Robert and Dorianne, Baudoin and Carys

Dark and Bright—Rhys and Annalise

The Winds of the Heavens—Rhun and Glain, Rhydderch and Isolda

Dance of Love—Izzy and Farah

Carried Away—Blythe and Dieter

Sweet Taste of Love—Aidan and Nolana

Wild Viking Princess—Ragna and Reider

Hearts and Crowns—Gallien and Peridotte

Fatal Truths—Alex and Elayne

Sinful Passions—Bronson and Grace; Rodrick and Swan

Series featuring the stories of the Viking ancestors of my Norman families
The Rover Bold—Bryk and Cathryn
The Rover Defiant—Torstein and Sonja
The Rover Betrayed—Magnus and Judith

Caledonia Chronicles (Scotland)
Book I Pride of the Clan—Rheade and Margaret
Book II Highland Tides—Braden and Charlotte
Book 2.5 Highland Dawn—Keith and Aurora (a Kindle Worlds book)
Book III Roses Among the Heather—Blair &Susanna, Craig & Timothea

The Von Wolfenberg Dynasty (medieval Europe)
Book 1 Loyal Heart—Sophia and Brandt
Book 2 Courageous Hearts—Luther and Francesca
Book 3 Faithful Heart—Kon and Zara

MYTH AND MYSTERY
The Taking of Ireland—Sibràn and Aislinn

17TH CENTURY
Highland Betrayal—Morgan and Hannah

Novellas
Maknab's Revenge—Ingram and Ruby
Passion's Fire—Matthew and Brigandine
Banished—Sigmar and Audra
Hungry Like De Wolfe—Blaise and Anne—Kindle

Worlds
 Unkissable Knight—Dervenn and Victorine

If you like stories with medieval breeds of dogs, you'll enjoy **If Love Dares Enough, Carried Away, Fatal Truths, Wild Viking Princess** and **The Taking Of Ireland**. If you have a soft spot for cats, read **Passion in the Blood** and **Haunted Knights**.

Looking for historical fiction centered on a certain region?
 English History—all Montbryce Legacy books
 Norman French History—all Montbryce Legacy books
 Crusades—A Man of Value
 Welsh History—Conquering Passion, Defiant Passion, Dark and Bright, The Winds of the Heavens
 Scottish History—Conquering Passion, A Man of Value, Sweet Taste of Love, Highland Betrayal, all books in the Caledonia Chronicles Series
 European History (Holy Roman Empire)—Carried Away, Loyal Heart, Courageous Heart, Faithful Heart
 Danish History—Wild Viking Princess
 Spanish History—Dance of Love
 Ireland—Dark Irish Knight, The Taking Of Ireland

If you like to read about historical characters:
 William the Conqueror—Conquering Passion, If Love Dares Enough, Defiant Passion
 William Rufus—A Man of Value
 Robert Curthose, Duke of Normandy—Passion in the Blood

Henry I of England—Passion in the Blood, Sweet Taste of Love, Haunted Knights, Hearts and Crowns

Heinrich V, Holy Roman Emperor—Carried Away

Vikings—Wild Viking Princess, The Rover Bold, The Rover Defiant, The Rover Betrayed

Kings of Aragon (Spain)—Dance of Love

The Anarchy (England) (Stephen vs. Maud)—Hearts and Crowns, Fatal Truths, Sinful Passions

James I of Scotland—Pride of the Clan

Jacobites & Mary, Queen of Scots—Highland Tides

Oliver Cromwell, Charles I, Charles II—Highland Betrayal

Into Time Travel? You'll enjoy the Caledonia Chronicles series.

84213439R00071

Made in the USA
San Bernardino, CA
05 August 2018